T0162849

COW COLLEGE BLUES

D.H. OLSEN

Order this book online at www.trafford.com
or email orders@trafford.com

Most Trafford titles are also available at major online book retailers.

© Copyright 2012 D.H. Olsen.
All rights reserved. No part of this publication may be reproduced, stored in a retrieval system, or transmitted, in any form or by any means, electronic, mechanical, photocopying, recording, or otherwise, without the written prior permission of the author.

This is a work of fiction. All of the characters, names, incidents, organizations, and dialogue in this novel are either the products of the author's imagination or are used fictitiously.

Printed in the United States of America.

ISBN: 978-1-4669-1424-7 (sc)
ISBN: 978-1-4669-1423-0 (e)

Trafford rev. 02/08/2012

 www.trafford.com

North America & international
toll-free: 1 888 232 4444 (USA & Canada)
phone: 250 383 6864 ♦ fax: 812 355 4082

Oh, ya can't get to heaven

On Yonge streetcar
Cuz a Yonge streetcar
Don't go that far.
I ain't gonna grieve
My Lord no more.

Verse from a YMCA summer camp song, circa 1951.

Prologue

The three H's had appeared as promised. No, not horny, hornier and horniest but the weather triplets, hot, hazy humid—a usual happening during mid-August in southern Ontario. Billy Carlsen, on a return trip from the IGA to fetch a quart of milk, had just walked into his family home. It was completely deserted. His mother and father were at work and his sister and grandmother were uptown because the local Chainway was having a sale. Most Items 40% Off. The add trumpeted proudly.

After closing the front door Billy noticed a spread of envelopes on the floor beneath the letter slot. He bent down to pick them up and much to his surprise they were all addressed to him. William Francis Carlsen had sent his high school transcripts into four different universities along with application forms for admittance to the lofty heights of academic pursuit. The acceptance or better-luck-next-time responses were now resting in his trembling hands. He opened each letter in turn and read the enclosed pages carefully. Western, Queens, McMaster no cigar, that left a solitary, thin thread of hope and there it was; Sowsbury Agricultural College, one of the three faculties at the University of Sowsbury, was inviting Bill to join the freshman class. An immediate reply was requested as lectures would begin the second week in September.

Billy was a little deflated by the refusal of the big three but then he remembered what his Uncle Ole would say: "Some of ur choices in life are kinda like a having a good dump. It's all about the process of elimination." Well, not exactly words to live by but it did make sense to Bill.

Mike Pearson was Prime Minister of Canada, John F. Kennedy occupied the White House, "Dr No", the first of the Bond flicks, was number one at the box office, four Liverpudlians whose first names were, John, Paul, George and Ringo, were about to invade North America , the Toronto Maple Leafs had captured the Stanley Cup and young Master Carlsen was on his way to College. *Alea iacta est eh?*

"This is where your Uncle Dunc's car left the road, it collided with that Hydro pole over there and he was thrown through the windshield. The police said that Dunc suffered a broken neck when he hit the ground. Killed him instantly," his father spoke softly, as the '59 Biscayne swept around a sharp bend halfway between Centreville and Sowsbury. Uncle Duncan McClean wasn't a blood relative, but a well loved family friend who'd boarded with them in the early fifties when they'd rented the old farmhouse on the Burnhamthorpe Road. The house was part of a one-hundred acre potato farm. All gone now, a victim of Toronto's urban sprawl that had oozed amoeba-like over the rich agricultural lands, excreting strip malls and subdivisions. Billy Carlsen glanced at the pine trees that grew tight against the road, and for a fleeting moment, could see Uncle Dunc's face reflected off the car's mud spattered passenger window. He remembered the thick Scottish accent and his favorite expression whenever Bill asked him about his days in the RAF. "Well laddie that's a very long story." Billy would then listen, wide-eyed, as Pilot Officer D. G. McClean conjured up Spitfires and Hurricanes, locked in deadly combat, twisting and turning about a contrail-dusted, Battle of Britain sky.

*

Billy's daydream was interrupted when his father coughed several times before asking, "What happens when we get to the University?"

"The letter I got said, we're supposed to report to the registrars office Pop," Bill stated confidently. After this brief exchange father and son drove on, quietly enjoying the pastoral views of woodlots, barns and silos that punctuated the rolling countryside. When they came to a full stop at the four corners of Sowsbury, Billy instructed his father to turn left. The royal blue Chevrolet was now heading, at a sedate twenty miles per hour, up a wide roadway lined with century old maples and towering beeches.

Near the end of the shaded, picturesque boulevard Harold Carlsen pulled into a parking spot directly across from the University's Administration building. Several seconds later a one-eyed monster, plastered to the side wall of its ivy covered bell tower, chimed twelve times.

*

Hogstroff Hall, the nerve centre of Sowsbury University, was constructed of rough cut limestone blocks and in profile resembled a gigantic battleship resting at dry dock. The massive, polished oak front doors were wide open. After entering the hallowed structure, Bill and his dad proceeded directly to the information counter. A grey haired old crone, seated on a high backed stool behind the imposing mahogany barricade that separated mere mortals from the chosen ones directing traffic at the Ivory Tower, peered menacingly over a pair of fly speckled granny glasses. "Your name young man?" she cackled.

"William Carlsen," Billy gulped uncomfortably.

"Ah yes, William Francis Carlsen," she snickered wickedly. "I suppose you and Donald O'Connor are friends."

He knew all about "Francis the Talking Mule" movies and took this in stride.

"Yes ma'am, and I can get you Don's autograph if you'd like." This took the terminally wrinkled, bun-tailed bat by surprise. Unable to offer a suitable reply, she handed Billy an envelope containing a meal ticket, a timetable and the key to his room on the third floor of Hereford Hall.

*

Father and son, each carrying a large suitcase, took the elevator to the top level of the residence and found room 301. The hardwood door, of his new home away from home, yawned invitingly and Bill walked straight in.

A solidly built, dark haired kid, standing in the middle of the room, smiled shyly while wiping his black, horn rimmed glasses. "Hi I'm Pete Eastman."

"Put her there Pete!" Billy grinned, as handshakes and further introductions were exchanged.

2

Pete helped to transport the rest of Bill's gear, and with the additional body, only one trip to the family chariot was required to move all of Master Carlsen's worldly goods into the upper reaches of the Hereford Hilton.

"I guess I'd better make tracks Billy; your mother's expecting me for supper."

"Okay Pop, thanks for the drive up here."

"Y-You take care Son, and give us a call next week when you're settled in."

"Sure thing Dad," Billy said reassuringly. He accompanied his father to the elevator, then returned to 301 to unpack.

*

"So where's home for you Pete?" Bill asked, while stuffing socks and underwear into the top drawer of an old mission oak dresser.

Before answering, Pete placed a forty-five on the turntable of a portable record player that he'd set up on his desk. It was a rock and roll piece by a new British group called the Beatles. The song had something to do with wanting to grab your hand, or an equally convenient appendage. This wasn't Bill's bag, he preferred folk music. In his tiny corner of the universe Peter, Paul and Mary ruled supreme.

"I'm from Mimico, that's in west TO," Pete answered, before adjusting the volume on his player.

"Hey, how about that, our Georgetown football team played an exhibition game against you guys last fall."

"Jeez, I had to cover that one for our Yearbook."

"Your defence were a hard nosed bunch, in the first half I sprained a finger and it bugged me all season."

"How come you chose Sowsbury?" Pete asked, changing the subject abruptly, football wasn't exactly number one on his Hit Parade.

"It was the only place that accepted me. Two years to complete my senior year and a borderline average wasn't enough to get me into Meds. eh?"

"Boy, you're lucky to be here."

"Tell me about it Pete."

3

The University of Sowsbury was one of the smallest institutions of higher education in the Province of Ontario. It was made up of three faculties. The Sowsbury Agricultural College or S.A.C., the Veterinary District College, or V.D.C. and the Flora Udderson College of Home Economics or F.U.C. Due to the nature of the courses and the lack of male equality in the year of our Lord nineteen-hundred and sixty-three, F.U.C. Home Ec. boasted an all female student body. This statistic suited the Vets and Aggies just fine.

*

Room 301 wasn't exactly a suite at the Royal York. The Spartan furnishings consisted of two dressers, two single beds, two desks, two wooden chairs and a small clothes closet, but it did have a killer view of the parking lot three floors below.

After stowing six pairs of socks into a top drawer, Bill felt his stomach begin to growl. "Hey Pete, I could use some chow."

"Yeah, me too. Why don't we head over to Barthman Hall and try out our new meal tickets."

"Sounds like a winner, Peter me good man," Billy showboated, while pulling the three square card from a well worn wallet.

*

The dinning Hall was located seventy yards from their residence. Most of the buildings on campus were constructed of limestone blocks, however, the trees and shrubs planted around the built-like-brick-shirt-house bunkers, softened the medieval look of this bastion of acedemic excellence.

There was already a line-up extending to the bottom steps outside Barfman—as it was affectionately known by the inmates of Sowsbury—when the neophyte roomies arrived on the scene. Bill spotted a pair of gorgeous Udderson girls just ahead of them. He couldn't resist, and gave them his standard ice breaker. "Gee wiz, this must be heaven because I'm standing behind two of the best looking angels in the universe."

4

"Give me a break Frosh, when you grow up and start shaving send us a letter," the taller of the maidens hissed, fixing Billy with a look that could have flash frozen a wooly mammoth. The cringing freshmen, too embarrassed to answer, kept their mouths shut and heads down. Billy discovered later that the F.U.C. lovelies were in their senior year and required no air freshener when they defecated.

Upon entering the back of the dinning hall Pete and Billy heard a swelling squeal of females chanting, "Double trouble, double tricks, were the babes from sixty-six." This was followed by an earthquake rumble of two-hundred baritone voices shouting, "Hey chicks we love those tricks, we're Aggies sixty-six."

It was a school tradition for each year to have it's own yell, or one in response to the another year's, so not to be out done, a thunderous explosion of male vocal chords bellowed, "Aggies are a bloody bore, yea Vets sixty four." All S.A.C. in the hall except for the freshmen countered with a rousing chorus that was sung to the tune of the old camp fire favorite, "Found a Peanut."

"We're Aggies, we're Aggies, we're Aggies, don't forget, and we'd rather be an Aggie than a dirty stinking Vet." There was no love lost between the two rival faculties. Bill and Pete along with three-hundred bewildered Frosh were year sixty-seven, and didn't have a yell, or really a clue as to what was going on.

Bill finally got to the serving area and looked apprehensively at the hot meal that was shoveled onto a heavy ceramic plate by a hair-netted, Viking Warrior Princess, wielding a long handled serving spoon. He hurriedly picked up a bowl of jello, spiked with pieces of fruit, then grabbed a selection of cutlery and a glass that looked like it had been liberated from a local motel. Billy flashed his shinny new meal ticket at the cashier seated on a stool near the end of the serving counter, and was directed to the large stainless steel containers in the middle of the hall which dispensed a tapped, white stream of homogenized moo.

The Sowsbury Agricultural College was very proud of its dairy herds. Quantity of milk was not a problem, so the policy was: 'drink till you drop'. "Too bad they didn't fill those cylinders with beer," William Francis muttered to himself, as he scoped out a place to deposit his tray. Bill found two empty seats near the end of one of the long dinning hall tables and waited for good roomie Eastman to park his butt.

*

Several minutes later, Pete carefully lowered himself onto a hard, grey metal chair next to Bill. Working patiently, like a paleontologist on a badlands dig, Pete scraped away a thick, gummy layer of rust-like sauce and slowly unearthed a circular object resting on the centre of his dinner plate. What he discovered wasn't a dinosaur egg, but a thinly sliced round of spongy material covered with something that looked a lot like sawdust.

"What in the hell is that?" Bill groaned loudly, when he saw the thing that Pete had uncovered.

An overgrown grizzly bear—masquerading as a full bearded senior—sitting directly across from them stopped shoveling mashed potatoes into the space below his nose and mumbled in a spud garbled voice, "That's mystery meat Frosh, eat it and it'll help you to grow fuzz on your balls."

After their run in with the Home Ec. lovelies, Billy was getting ticked by the freshmen put downs and snarled, "I guess that's how you managed to get the hair that normally grows wild around your arsehole to stick to your face."

Bill could see red hot rage begin to flare in the senior's eyes, but it suddenly disappeared. The gigantic upperclassman threw back his head before splitting the air with a thunderous laugh. "Hey, that's pretty good for a kid still wet behind the ears. My name's Charlie Ross and welcome to Hay Seed U."

He extended his huge paw across the table and nearly shook Bill's arm off. Charlie was one of the starting defensive tackles for the Sowsbury Woodchucks and asked Bill if he'd ever played ball.

6

"Yeah, I was on our high school team. I'd really like to be a Woodchuck, but with my marks, I'll sure as shootin' flunk out if I can't hit the books like gangbusters first term." "You know what S.A.C means for a Frosh who doesn't do his fair share of scabbing?" The big tackle smiled impishly. "Okay, I'll bite," Billy replied.

"Sacked At Christmas!" Charlie snorted, as a spitball sized chunk of mashed potato collided with Pete's forehead.

Pete gave Charlie a lopsided grin, then returned to carving up his slab of mystery meat. Billy, however, was painfully aware of Perry Como crooning "Home For the Holidays", and a blurry image of former Frosh Carlsen, clutching a bus ticket stamped one-way. Charlie abruptly excused himself, stating he had a heavy date with an F.U.C. beauty, before lumbering like a D7 bulldozer towards the red exit sign at the back of Barfman.

*

Just before bedtime, William Francis was about to open the door to 301—Pete standing beside him—when he heard the words which most Canadian males would consider the best thing to be offered to them, other than having sex with Sophia Loren."Would you guys like a beer?"

Bill did a rapid about face and trying not to drool, stammered, "G-God, I could kill for a cold one."

Ed Samson, a muscular, blond haired, six foot, two-hundred pound, pack-a-dayer, blinking from a blast of Craven 'A' smoke attacking his clear blue eyes, extended a farm toughened right hand. After the hi-how-are-ya's were completed, Pete being of good Baptist stock, mumbled something about a letter home before slowly shuffling towards the sanctuary of his new digs.

"I thought having beer in residence was against the rules," Bill whistled softly, while ogling the Marilyn Monroe calendar hanging over Ed's bed.

"Yep, according to the Sowsbury sacred code of ethics that's how it is," Eddie chuckled, before reaching into a red, metal Coke cooler to extract a matched pair of Bradings.

7

Ed then grabbed a church key and snapped the caps. "Boy is this ever good," Bill exhaled slowly, after a satisfying swallow. In his minds eye he could see the old bartender on the "Gillette Cavalcade of Sports" polishing the mahogany surface of his empire, before downing a frosty mug of Pabst Blue Ribbon.

"Yeah, the fact that it's strictly *verboten* makes it taste even better," Ed replied, taking another pull on the stubbie.

"You know, with no boze and no broads in the dorms we'll have to live like friggin' monks," Billy griped.

Ed smiled wickedly. "If you don't get caught, you can live any way you want."

Bill wasn't too sure about that one, but he was really enjoying the beer. "Holy cow, look at the time, and I've an early one tomorrow."

"An eight o'clock?"

"Yeah, Organic Chemistry over in the Biology building, according to the timetable they gave us."

"Me too." Ed fought to keep his eyelids from drooping. "Well Billy, I don't mean to be rude, but I'm about as worn out as a tomcat on a pussy cruise."

Bill guffawed loudly before saying, "Nice meeting you Eddie, and thanks for the barley sandwich." Yawning contentedly, he offered a friendly, over-the-shoulder wave on the way back to his room.

Pete had already hit the sack. Bill, trying his best not to disturb the mummy-like creature tightly wrapped in crisp white sheets on the bed across from him, undressed quickly before slipping under the covers.

"Holy doodle, I never thought I'd ever make it to College," Billy murmured softy in the general direction of his roommate, who was already snoring like a well oiled chain saw. William Francis Carlsen, who'd just turned twenty, was now a first year Aggie. He sighed happily, rolled over onto his side and went lights out, quietly ascending into a land where dreams came true and fair, buxom maidens catered willingly to your every desire.

8

2

*

The Barthman first call to breakfast was at six-thirty. Bill and Pete, hungrier than a pair of chipmunks in April, sat down to a generous serving of bacon and eggs moments after the clock tower chimed seven times. The only downside to the meal was the sickly sweet coffee that tasted like a urine sample from a diabetic horse. Billy managed to choke down the offending liquid, but made a mental note to order tea the next day. They finished up at seven-thirty and were on time for the Organic Chemistry class that started at eight.

*

The spacious lecture hall was filled to capacity with first year Aggies, Vets and Udderson girls. A professor wearing a crisp, clean, full length, white lab. coat entered through a green, metal side door and made his way to the raised platform located at bottom dead centre of the roomy amphitheater. After clearing his throat, he projected in deep resonant tones, "Good morning ladies and gentlemen, my name's Dr. Robinson."

Bill leaned over to Pete and inquired in a dulcet whisper, "Why would an M.D. be teaching Organic Chemistry?"

Pete rolled his eyes before muttering, "He's a PH.D. you turkey, and they get the Doctor title along with the degree." This seemed to satisfy Bill, and he settled back to see what this guy, without the stethoscope, would say.

Professor Robinson looked around the hall before pontificating knowingly, "I want each of you to look at the person to your left, now look at the person to your right." Everyone did as they were told wondering where this was going.

"Statistics show that one of the three of you will fail their first term and not be allowed to return after Christmas."

"Did ya hear that?" Pete hissed. "Charlie was right S.A.C.—Sacked At Christmas."

Dr. Robinson then began to read from his prepared notes and by the end of the hour, Bill's head was spinning.

What in the hell's an aromatic hydrocarbon anyway, was all William Francis could think about when the good doctor's lips stopped moving. *Maybe it's a sweet smelling lump of wet coal or something.*

Two terminally bewildered roommates rushed out of the large lecture theatre and hustled their buns to a 9:15 Physics class. Another sixty minutes—of trying to figure out what the guy at the front was talking about—zoomed on by before Pete and Bill double timed it over to the Biology Building for a 10:30 Botany lecture. Shortly before noon, a matched pair of stunned freshman, barely running on the fumes, made their way to the dinning hall.

On the steps of Barthman they noticed two Home Ec. girls ahead of them. Since there were only three females in the S.A.C. and two in the V.D.C., then anything wearing skirts was likely F.U.C.—although, a very disturbed Aggie of the circle and arrow gender might have been a remote possibility. The previous days rejection still loomed large in Billy's mind, so he said nothing. One of the girls, a very attractive brunette, glanced their way and smiled. "I saw you two guys at the Orgies lecture. Pretty scary stats eh?"

By Orgies Bill realized she meant Organic Chemistry and not some depraved exhibition that he would have given his left nut to witness.

"Yeah, it kinda gives a whole new meaning to, "I'll Be Home For Christmas," Pete answered ruefully.

The girls giggled in unison, and displaying a sparkling Pepsident smile, the good looking blonde with the bouffant cooed seductively, "We're two of Flora's newest recruits, I guess you're Frosh too."

Bill grinned. "Yep, green as grass, baby fresh, mother-trucking rookies of this here fine Cow College."

Pete, hoping that Billy had really said trucking, did the introductions. Margaret Parsons, the dark haired beauty and Jane Armstrong the blonde goddess, replied in kind.

Jane looked directly at Bill before asking, "Are you and Pete attending Young Peoples on Thursday night?"

"I-I'm not very religious, so I-I think I'll stay home and hit the books," William Francis stammered.

The two girls did a double take. Margaret seeing the look of confusion on Billy's face said, "Young Peoples is held at the Empire Hotel. The girls gather in the Ladies and Escorts and the guys usually wander over from the Men's Beverage Room to say hello."

The pubs were still segregated in the fall of '63, and they closed between six and eight, so that working men would get home for supper. For a guy to be on the L&E side, he had to be sitting at the same table with a female of the species, one that he'd escorted there, or one who'd invited him to her table.

Bill's only experience with Young Peoples was at the United Church in Georgetown. He'd attended these meetings with his girlfriend Doris Marshall. Reverend Willard Wrighteous, protector of the faith and spearhead of the 'Dry' vote sure as hell hadn't offered anyone a beer.

Billy smiled self consciously before admitting, "I'm a little shy of the magic twenty-one. I'd be tossed out on my ear if I tried to get served at a hotel."

Jane looked at Bill as if he was a card carrying goody-two-shoes. "Well then, borrow someone's ID who's legal age and won't be there."

"If you really want to go Billy, use my birth certificate. I turned twenty-one in July, and I'll be scabbing in the library Thursday evening."

"Hey thanks Pete, you're a real pal."

They were at the cashiers station by now and each of them had selected soup, ham sandwich, and a slice of blueberry pie. The girls wanted to sit with some of their classmates, so Pete and Bill said good-bye and found a table.

"I didn't want to say it when the girls were around, but the truth is; my family are members of the Baptist Church, and we're strict teetotalers."

"I guess you won't be needing your ID very much this year eh?" Bill grinned winningly, seeing the possibilities.

11

"No sweat Billy, use it whenever you want."

This brought on a deja vu moment for young master Carlsen. He'd spent a summer up in the Muskokas two years ago, and used to borrow a fake ID from a guy he worked with. Billy had just turned eighteen, but he was able to buy beer, and had a bootlegging business going on the side.

"Gee, thanks roomie."

Pete reached into his billfold, extracted a wallet sized, newly laminated, birth certificate and handed it to Bill. Sure enough, one Peter Martin Eastman was born on July the thirty-first, nineteen-forty-two.

"Where'd the Martin come from?"

"That's my dad's name."

"How about that, I know exactly what I'm going to call you from now on."

"I'm almost afraid to ask."

"Spin, as in Spin and Marty."

"Oh yeah, the Mickey Mouse Club . You know I've been called worse by better."

"Hey Spin," Pete winced noticeably at the unwelcome nickname. "speaking of Mouseketeers and all, do you remember Davy Crockett."

"Yep, I used to watch that Disney series in the fifties. I wonder what Fess Parker and Buddy Ebsen are doing today? I'll bet they're not wearing coon skin caps."

"You know Spin, when I was in grade eight back in good old Georgetown, I had a rusty car radio antenna clamped to the handle bars of my bike. Just below the little bead at the top, I had a raccoon tail tied on with a piece of waxed string."

"Jeez Billy, you must've been a real cool cat back in those days."

"Yeah Spin, just like ice cream, but I can still see myself riding around while I was delivering the *Toronto Star* singing: "Davy, Davy Sprocket, he oiled his chain with beer.""

"Hold the fort a minute Carlsen, have you got a drivers licence?" Pete groaned, when he heard the fractured lyrics.

"Sure do, had it since I was seventeen."

"That's real neat Billy. My dad wouldn't let me drive until I was eighteen. Is it okay if I have a look at it?"

Bill reached into his wallet, pulled out the prized document, then carefully placed it on the edge of the long dinning room table. Pete grabbed the folded piece of paper and after several moments of intense concentration he began to smile.

"You know what William Francis Carlsen, I've got the perfect nickname for you. How does Mule sound?"

"I guess you weren't too impressed by Spin eh? I'll make a deal, no more Mule and no more Spin. Okay?"

"Sold American!" Pete yodelled happily.

"Yeah, LSMFT: Lucky Strike Means Fine Tobacco, then again, as they used to say up in the Muskokas, Loose Sweaters Mean Floppy Tits." Billy delivered a slow wink.

*

Since Laboratory classes weren't scheduled for the afternoon the former Spin and Mule, clutching typed lists in their hands, wandered down to the campus bookstore on Holstein Avenue where they gathered up Chemistry, Zoology, Botany, Calculus, Physics and English texts. By the time the weary Frosh got back to Hereford, their arms had stretched an inch from the heavy load of academia. Reading assignments had been dished out like a harvest stew, motivating the two roomies to pursue a modicum of paper perusal before supper.

*

The evening meal was uneventful. After a bowl of silage salad and a Swiss steak—that had been hardened to a iron like finish two weeks ago in Switzerland—Pete headed off to a 'Christian's for Christ' meeting, while Billy returned to the residence, and attempted to decode the secret messages cleverly hidden in his Physics text. He'd started to yawn, and was about to assume the horizontal when Ed Samson barged through the door.

"Get off your royal duff Carlsen, we're going to paint the canon!" Eddie bellowed like a roaring lion.

13

A large canon stood proudly on a cement pad in front of Yorkshire Hall, the University's library. It was a time honoured tradition for the freshman to paint it orange and yellow—the official school colors. In addition, the year of graduation would be dispalyed in bold brush strokes on the barrel. Ed and Billy arrived at the art show just as a group of Frosh were putting the finishing touches on the wheels of the old artillery piece. The year sixty-seven Aggies, grouped tightly around the ancient gun, failed to notice a gaggle of stealthy sophomores—each carrying a metal waste basket filled to the brim with water—about to make a bombing run. The sixty-sixers caught the wannabe Van Goghs off guard, and managed to soak them from head to toe before you could say cowabunga.

The crowing second year firemen then scampered into the darkness shouting unkind things about the intelligence and dubious ancestry of the freshmen class. By the time the painters and spectators had recovered it was too late to give chase. It was getting cold and the water, slowly seeping into to shoes and underwear, made it even colder. A collective no brainer prompted,the wet as drowned cat rookies, to hurry back to Hereford in order to dry off and warm up.

*

Billy was about to get into bed when Ed knocked on the door and invited William Francis to step into the hallway.

"I've got a plan," Ed whispered

"For what?" Billy rasped apprehensively

"Pay back time, here's how it works. I'm a bit of a Chemistry nut, and I just happen to have the ingredients for a stink bomb."

"So what good's that?" Bill absently scratched his head.

"I'm setting my alarm for three, then I'm going to sneak over to Jersey Hall where most of the sophomores live."

"Yeah, and then what Eddie?"

"I mix some iron sulfide from my old Chemistry set with a dash of muriatic acid and golly whiz Mr. Science, just like magic, you've got rotten egg gas."

14

"So where do I come in?" Billy shrugged.

"I kinda need a lookout while doing my Chem101 project, and I was hoping...."

"Okay, I hate being bullied by a bunch of prima dona Sophs, count me in."

When Bill got back to his room Pete was already sawing logs, therefore, no explanation was necessary.

*

Billy was sleeping lightly when he heard a gentle tapping at the door. He got up and dressed quickly. Once outside, the two hell-bent-for-revenge Frosh, hugged the shadows until they reached Jersey Hall. They quietly entered the residence and noticed that no one was in the common room, located just to the right of the main door.

"B-Billy stand by the stairwell, you should be able to see the entrance from there. If anyone comes down the stairs, or in the front door, give a low whistle," Ed croaked, his voice barely above a whisper.

"No way Eddie, I'll be a dead duck if that happens."

"Relax Carlsen, tell them you're new on campus and you've just come back from a steamy date, then ask how to get to Hereford Hall."

" O-Okay," Billy quavered, "but it sounds fishy to me."

Ed disappeared into the common room carrying a brown paper bag. He took out a small bottle containing black iron sulfide powder, and poured its contents into a soup bowl he'd liberated from Barthman. He then added the acid, and carefully placed the bowl under a large couch. Eddie tiptoed to where Bill was waiting and pointed towards the door.

*

They made their way back to the residence, very quietly ascended the side stairs, then walked cautiously along the hallway to Ed's room. It was one of the few singles in Hereford and he didn't have a roommate. His tiny window looked across the parking lot to the main entrance of Jersey. It took about half an hour for the gas to diffuse into the rooms on the first and second floor.

15

Shortly thereafter, and much to the amusement of the two budding Chemists, a steady stream of coughing, sneezing, sleepy heads began to mill about on the sidewalk in front of the dorm. It was just about shooting light when the Firemen found the "bomb" under the couch where Eddie had left it. Bill and his partner in crime never breathed a word to anyone about the incident, but the Aggies of sixty-six had watched enough Dragnet reruns to know that it was likely a freshman revenge project. Surprisingly enough, on that same night, the President of the sophomore class had his car doors painted yellow and orange. Frosh two, Sophs one: was the way the boys of '67 scored it.

16

It was a red eyed, sorry assed Billy Carlsen who stumbled into his eight o'clock Zoology lecture the next morning. He'd skipped breakfast to be there on time. The day had turned out to be sunny-blue, but all this was lost on the lookout guy. Calculus followed by Botany rounded out his pre-lunch timetable. Still half-asleep, William Francis choked down a hot beef sandwich at Barfman, then returned to the dorm to crash for an hour before rushing off to a Physics Lab.

By the early evening Bill was on the ropes, but figured he still had enough steam to crack an English book. He wasn't very enthusiastic about reading Chaucer, but it had to be done. The text was written in Middle English with translation notes in the margins. He'd just about had enough of "Cranberry Tales"—as Pete liked to call them— when Eddie sauntered into 301. Good Aggie Eastman was over at Yorkshire attending a 'Holier Than Thou' seminar, so Billy was home alone.

"I guess we showed those dipsticks from six-six eh?"

"Yeah, but that's our secret. Right?" Bill affirmed.

"For sure partner. Hey, it's Thursday!"

"Are you queer or something?" Billy raised his eyebrows.

"Oh, I get it, Thursday, fruits day. Take it easy Carlsen, it's Young Peoples at the pub and I think we should check it out."

Bill thought it over for a moment, then walked over to Pete's dresser and took out the wallet sized birth certificate that his roommate had left in the top drawer.

Billy smiled, before presenting Mr. Geoffrey Chaucer a farewell finger. "Yeah, I could use a beer."

Ed had his own car, a '56 Volkswagen. They climbed aboard the Bug and drove the short distance to downtown Sowsbury. Eddie found a parking spot right beside the Men's Entrance of the Empire Hotel and nosed the Beetle between the white lines. The beverage room was crammed, wall to wall, with Vets and Aggies, but they were able to locate a recently vacated table near the bar.

As if by magic a waiter appeared carrying a tray packed with glasses of draught beer. "Ale or lager boy's?"

"A-Ale for me," Billy wheezed, looking around for the long arm of the law.

"Make mine lager," Ed replied confidently. *See no evil fear no evil.*

Bill handed the waiter a folded one eyed Queen and deepening his voice, gestured to the change on the table, "Take one for yourself."

When the beer slinger was out of ear shot Eddie orated like an old pro, "If we tip him every round, I don't think we'll get hassled for ID."

"I sure hope you're right Samson, but if a cop comes in we're outta here."

After his fourth goblet of suds Billy was feeling adventurous, and decided to take a quick look on the Ladies and Escorts side. His heart did a flip when he spotted two knock-down beauties sitting at a table by the door. One was a redhead and the other a strawberry blonde. Bill gathered up his courage and went over to say hello.

They were Home Ec. types from sixty-six, but didn't seem upset that Bill was a freshman. He mentioned that he was with a friend. The girls conferred by a simple nod, before asking Bill to go fetch Eddie. One minute later two matched pairs were seated around a small table on the L&E side. The redhead, who seemed to be in a very good mood, introduced herself and the strawberry blonde.

"My name's Judy Lawson and this is my roommate Gail Taylor."

"Hey, pleased to meet you, I'm Ed Samson and the good looking curly haired, brown eyed, five-ten, one- hundred and eighty pounder is my best buddy Billy Carlsen."

Gail chortled appreciatively, but wanting to make Sow U small talk, she bubbled like a gossip at a tea party, "Did you guys hear about the stink bomb last night?"

"Just a rumor this morning during breakfast," Bill said, looking like an alter boy assisting at communion.

18

"Gary Barker's car doors were painted orange and yellow too," Gail tut-tutted.

"Who's this Barker guy anyway?" Ed coughed, while lighting up a Craven A.

"Gary's the President of second year Aggies and the best hockey player on campus," Judy gushed. "Gosh, he's so cute."

"Is Gary from Brampton?" Bill asked.

"He used to play Junior 'B' hockey there," Gail all but swooned.

"I know who you mean," Ed said, while inhaling another lungful. "I saw him in a game back in St. Thomas when he was still playing Junior 'C'. He sure is a slick centre."

"Yeah, I used to get over to Brampton when he played for the 7 UP'S," Billy added. "You know, he had a chance to move up to the Marlboros but turned it down in order to attend College."

"Wow! A lot of guys from the Marlies have gone on to the Leaf's eh?" Ed exclaimed, an obvious note of awe in his voice.

"Well, I heard that Gary's invited the entire freshman year to a car painting party on Saturday at the Bear Flag. It's kind of a hatchet burying bash," Judy said sweetly, while innocently reaching under the table and brushing Bill's knee.

"Where the heck's this Bear Flag?" Billy gulped, feeling the electric touch of Judy's hand.

"Five Aggies from sixty-six rented an old farmhouse down in Cowplop Township, you drive five miles south on forty-nine and hang a right," Judy replied brightly, looking directly into Billy's widening eyes.

"But why the Bear Flag?" Eddie asked.

"Apparently the guys are studying "Cannery Row" in English 201 and they took the name for their place from Stienbeck's novel," Gail informed the two Frosh.

"Hey, that's a good one," Bill gasped , as Judy's fingers began to meander north of his kneecap.

"Is this an inside joke?" Eddie frowned, feeling left out.

"Listen up Samson," Bill lectured. "The Bear Flag was a house of ill or well repute, depending on your point of view."

"Oh, a whorehouse!" Ed enthused, forgetting himself for a moment. "Shoot! Excuse me ladies, I forgot my manners."
"Don't sweat it Eddie I'm not Margaret Anderson and Judy isn't exactly Harriet Nelson," Gail soothed, a trace of motherly amusement in her voice—these, after all, were Home Economics majors.
"You know Billy you kinda remind me of a Teddy Bear I used to have years ago," Judy mimicked, in her best Annette Funicello voice.

*

Oh my God! This bear thing will never leave me alone, Bill thought to himself. When he'd worked up north two summers ago one of his nicknames was Teddy. It seemed that every card carrying female could see this bruin image whenever they looked at young William Francis.

*

"So, what time does the car painting party start on Saturday ?" Billy blushed slightly, steering them away from the baby bear stuff.
"Beats me," Judy answered, the tips of her fingers now inches away from the Carlsen crown jewels. "I'm getting all this second hand."

*

Another round of suds appeared on the table, then another. A time warp must have taken place at the Empire, because a full micro-blink later their waiter announced loud and clear, "Last round folks."
"Holy smoke, "Bill squeaked, as Judy suddenly removed her hand from his inner thigh. "it's just about midnight."
"What's the matter Teddy does your coach turn into a pumpkin at the bewitching hour?" Judy mocked gently.
"No, but eight o'clock Orgies is going to be a killer."
"Time to make like the Lone Ranger and blow this pop stand, " Ed opined, while fumbling around for his car keys.
They piled into the Bug, and by the grace of whoever looks after drunks and lost puppies, made it back to the safety of Hereford in one piece.

"Hey Gail you wanna come up to my room for a quickie? Whoops, I mean night-cap." Ed grinned wolfishly. The rule book had been thrown out the window, and caution was gone with the wind.

Bill seeing his role in the unfolding drama stage whispered, "How bout I walk you back to Udderson Hall; Judy, Judy, Judy." *Cary Grant, eat your heart out.*

*

Ed and Gail, hand in hand, trying their best to suppress an attack of the giggle fits, disappeared through the side door of the residence. Bill put his arm around Judy's shoulder, and encountering no resistance, suggested they start their trek to, Chickville, Skirt City, Babeland, or in the immortal words of Jessie James, Posse Galore.
We'll see you later Norm, down by the girl's dorm.

*

Ten yards away from the hallowed steps of Our Lady of Perfect Pastries, Judy purred seductively, "There's a deking bush over there Teddy."

"Are you a horticulture type or something?" *Who cares about a dumb nickname anyway. As long as she thinks it's cute and I get a little honey, what the hey!*

Remembering she was talking to a Frosh, Judy chuckled, "No silly, that's a small clump of shrubs where members of the opposite sex go when they want to make out, or as my grandmother would say spark."

Bill eyed the patch of vegetation that Judy was pointing at. "Terrific! I've always wanted to be a Bushologist."

Judy turned out to be anything but a tease. Once they were behind the dense cover of a tall cedar hedge she unzipped Bill's fly and demonstrated her farm raised talents as a milkmaid. Bill returned the favour in a most gentlemanly fashion and when the earth stopped shaking he politely wished Judy a sweet visit with the sandman.

*

Several minutes later, while passing by Eddie's room, Billy stopped for a moment and stood perfectly still.

21

Pressing his ear against the cold varnished surface of the wooden door, he heard soft moans and attenuated squeals of orgasmic delight coming from the comfy depths of the inner sanctum. Realizing what he was doing, Billy quickly straightened up and tiptoed towards 301. *Holy smokers, I'm turning into a Listening Tom.*

4

*

Pete attempted to get his roommate out of the sack, but it was like trying to raise the *Titanic*. Billy was unable to answer the bell and returned to a deep dreamless sleep. When he finally unwrapped the covers, glued to his head, it was nine-thirty and he'd already missed two lectures. William Francis, in a panic, leaped from the pit, dressed quickly, then headed for the Physics building .

*

He arrived just in time to make the ten o'clock. A booming pile driver hammered against the inflamed lining of his swollen brain, and a extremely nasty, nocturnal camel had deposited a reeking desert chip in his mouth. Listerine couldn't help this case of terminal halitosis.

Bill was the first to admit that he wasn't God's gift to the academic world. Two years to complete his senior year and barely squeezing through a crack in the side door of the S.A.C., did *not* make him a major threat for a scholarship. This meant survival at the ivory tower would require: nose to the grid stone, shoulder to wheel, burning the midnight oil, giving one-hundred and ten percent. *Ruckin'* fight *eh?*

He slumped down next to Pete and rasped, "Thanks for trying to get me out of bed, but I was too pooped to participate."

"What time did you roll in?"

"Well after midnight," Bill muttered, as the lecture began.

*

Billy's stomach was doing back-springs, but he did manage to keep his lunch down and made it over to the Physical Education building for the last class of the day. After everyone had changed into shorts and running shoes, they were ordered by the instructor to report to the football field.

The Woodchucks were away at McMaster playing the Marauders, so the freshmen had the field all to themselves. Instead of footballs the guy with the whistle, Dr. Hamish McJock, had a bag full of rugby balls slung over his shoulder.

Using various members of the class to demonstrate, he introduced them to scrums, line-outs and the technique of lateral passing. They also practiced drop kicking and tackling. It was a warm September afternoon and Bill had a great time. The exercise helped to clear up the remnants of a Red Cap overdose and he began to feel human again. At three-thirty the Frosh were told to hit the showers, and just after four Bill headed for the residence.

He met Ed Samson near the door of 301 and stopped to shoot the breeze.

"Did you make it to any lectures at all today Eddie?" He knew for sure that his drinking buddy wasn't at Phys. Ed.

"Nope, had to catch up on my beauty sleep. After the stink bomb, and Young Peoples last night, I was one tired puppy come the wee hours."

"You and Gail hit it off pretty good eh?"

"Well, let's just say that Miss Taylor is a blue ribbon specimen of young Canadian womanhood, and a credit to the fine school of Household Science located on this here campus."

"Cut the crap Eddie, did you score or what?"

"Billy, I'm offended you'd ask such a personal question?"

"Okay Romeo, for the time being we'll let that one alone, how about some chow?"

"William my fine feathered friend, now you're talking my language."

*

Friday night supper at Barthman featured roast pork, mashed potatoes with gravy, peas, carrots and apple pie a la mode for desert. Bill figured that Queen Elizabeth must have arrived on campus. His royal theory was blown apart when a junior informed him that the President of the Porcine Palace ate at the dinning hall every once in a while, and tonight was the night.

After they sat down, Ed looked around for Mr. Big but couldn't locate him.

"I guess his arse-holiness will be here later," Bill quipped.

"Yeah, I wonder if he likes mystery meat?"

"No way, he may be top banana but he's not crazy. Hey Eddie, a splashy flier on the third floor bulletin board said "The Birds" is playing at the local beanery."

"So you wanna take in a flick Billy?"

"Spot on Sherlock, I'm in the mood for a night at the picture show."

*

At six-thirty the freshmen movie buffs piled into Eddie's Volks and headed for the Roxy. They loaded up on popcorn and Cokes, then found a pair of seats down front. The Hitchcock thriller was a gripper. Bill wasn't overly impressed by Tippi Hedren—who'd have a name like Tippi anyway. He did, however, think that Suzanne Pleshette would make a great snuggy. As soon as the film ended and while the animated characters on screen were singing, "Let's all go to the lobby to get ourselves a treat", Ed and Bill scrambled for the exit.

Shortly after emerging into the cool night air; Eddie paused for a moment and pointed across the street, "How about we go over to the Grand Central for a beer."

"Only if you twist my arm," Bill groaned, while jamming the back of his wrist against the small of his back.

The draught room was half-full, so they had no problem finding a table. The waiter plunked down four glasses of suds and didn't even ask for ID when they tipped: "one for himself". Bill looked around the room and noticed a tall, square jawed, athletic type decked out in a brand new leather Aggie Jacket. He could see from the numbers sown on to the right sleeve that the arm inside was from year sixty-six. The other arm waved at them, before the jacket with body attached came over to their table.

"You guys go to the Ag. college?" The head above the collar asked.

"We're Frosh," Ed replied proudly.

"Well in that case welcome to the S.A.C. Mind if I join you?"

Bill gestured toward an empty chair. "Take a load off your feet."

"Ed Samson and Billy Carlsen," Ed said, pointing in the appropriate directions.

"Gary Barker," the sophomore replied.

"Hey, how about that! I've seen you play hockey at Memorial Arena in Brampton."

"Yeah, I was lucky enough to make the team a couple of years ago."

"Are you in residence?" Eddie asked.

"Yep, Jersey Hall."

Bill beamed seraphically. "Being new on campus we only know where Hereford is."

"Well, if you look across your back parking lot, Jersey's the first building on the left."

"Are you heading home this weekend?" Ed shifted uneasily, wanting to guide things away from a discussion of the "bomb".

"Nope, I'm sticking around, and if you guys are interested, come down to the Bear Flag Saturday for a car painting party."

"Yeah, we heard about that at Young Peoples," Bill responded innocently.

"We also heard that it was your wheels," Eddie commiserated.

"My Fairlane's a bit of a mess, but it'll look a lot better by Sunday."

"You can count on us to be there," Bill affirmed.

"Hey, it's been nice meeting you guys, but I'm off to do some serious scabbing."

"Have a good one eh?" Eddie waved, as Gary pushed through the pub door.

"Boy, is he ever a good shit!"

"Carlsen you're a fine judge of character, and fer sure, we'll check out the scene at this here Cowplop cat house," Ed twanged, in his best Sow U accent.

Billy curled his thumb and index finger. "In like Flynn."

26

On Saturday morning Bill and Pete arrived at Barthman in time for the last call to breakfast. After a simple meal of corn flakes, tea and a bran muffin they returned to 301. Pete stayed in the dorm to study while Bill took a walk around campus. He was passing by Udderson when he noticed a gorgeous brunette, sitting on a park bench opposite the residence. Figuring she was a new student, like himself, he stopped to say hello.

"A-Are you waiting for Christmas?" Bill stuttered, totally captivated by the girl on the bench.

The dark haired beauty smiled guardedly. "Are you one of Santa's helpers?"

"No, I was just reminded of the line from a song, you know, chestnuts toasting on the open Bunsen burner, or something like that. It's the first thing I thought of when I saw you sitting there."

The raven haired princess looked at Bill skeptically. "Frosh huh?"

"Yeah, but you're new here too, right?"

"F.U.C. sixty-five Rudolph."

"Whoops, I kinda goofed on that one, my name's Billy Carlsen."

"Hello there Billy, I'm Donna Parker."

"So where's home Donna."

"Port Carter, a small town in the Muskokas, you've probably never heard of it."

"Holy commoly! Does your Dad run the A&P in the Port?"

"How'd you know that?" Donna gasped audibly.

"Two summers ago, I did a guest appearance up there as a short-order cook at the Hilltop Café."

"So you worked for Paul Evans."

"I sure did. Hey, what's Doc Livingstone up to these days?"

"Doc's sort of a celebrity at home. Last summer he water skied from Kingston to Quebéc City, the story was in the *Star Weekly*."

"Well good for the Doc. I know that skiing a big river was one of his dreams."

27

Bill recalled that Ian Livingstone, the town's milkman and a Pat Boone doppelganger, wanted to ski down the Mississippi all the way to New Orleans, but what the heck, *La Ville de Québec* was just as good.

The boy meets girl duo, continued to chat away about mutual acquaintances for an hour or more. Suddenly realizing the time Billy stood up quickly. "Donna it's been great getting caught up and all, but I've gotta scoot. Me and my buddy are driving down to the Bear Flag to play Rembrandt, so I'd best be on my way."

"It's not everyday I meet someone who knows the Port as well a you do. I hope we can talk again," Donna cooed, a frank look of interest in her eyes.

*

Bill was only in his room for ten minutes when Ed tapped on the door. "You ready to go?"

"Ready Teddy to rock 'n' roll," Billy chuckled. "but let's grab a bite at the dinning hall before we point her south."

They were served the Saturday lunch standard, chipped beef on toast. Billy eyeballed the gourmet special on his plate and moaned, "You know, my Uncle Ole told me when he was in the army they called this SOS; shit on a shingle."

Ed for some strange reason had lost his appetite and couldn't finish the brown gooey mass set before him.

*

They arrived at the Cowplop farm shortly after one. Sure enough, there on top of a white flagpole was a banner with a bear printed on it's surface. Bill found out latter that this was the state flag of California. A large group of students were gathered around a fifty-five Fairlane. The windows, bumpers, head lights, and tail lights, had been neatly covered. There was a sign next to the car that read: TWENTY MINUTES OF PAINTING: TWENTY-FIVE CENTS: *Kind of reminds you of Tom Sawyer*, Bill thought. The money was to defray the cost of materials.

Bill wandered over to the car, and flipped a quarter into a soup can before grabbing a brush.

Ed did the same and when their allotted time was up they had the doors covered with a brilliant yellow lacquer. A steady stream of would-be Tom Thomsons did a passable job of painting the rest of the Fairlane. The car was now a mobile symbol of school spirit, since the hood, roof and trunk lid were painted bright orange and the rest of the car was decked out in canary yellow. Four cases of beer and several hours later the Frosh and Sophs had signed an unofficial truce. Gary Barker's chariot was now, without a doubt, the numero uno jalopy on campus.

29

5

The farmhouse at the Bear Flag was a classic Cowplop beauty: large kitchen, summer kitchen, front parlor and dinning room on the main floor—five bedrooms and a bathroom filled in the second floor. The Aggies who lived there were all planning to go into the Wildlife Biology option in the second term. Gary Barker, being the year President, was good friends with the inmates of the Flag, and it was their idea to hold the car decorating day. Bill was sitting in a rag-a-muffin easy chair, sipping on a cold beer, when Gary came into the spacious parlor.

*

"Thanks for showing up Billy, you and Ed got things going."

"Did you cover you're costs?"

"Yeah, we broke even, and I'm up a paint job."

"Well, that's only fair considering what they did to your doors."

Gary chuckled before saying, "You're from Georgetown eh?"

"Yep, but we get over to Brampton every now and again. I was to your dad's store a couple of times to buy hockey equipment when I played pee-wee and bantam."

"I worked there all through high school, could be I even sold you something. You know, my old man's okay, this summer for instance, he gave me a trip to Europe for passing first year."

"Hey, how about that, I got across the pond too. Nothing fancy just youth hostels and hitch hiking." Bill's dad worked for Trans-Canada-Airlines and family members were eligible for flight passes anywhere that TCA flew.

"Boy is that ever something. I did just about the same thing."

"Get down to Greece?" Billy asked. "That was my favorite country."

"I made it as far as Athens, then took a local ferry over to the Island of Mykonos."

"Holy Toledo, I was there in July! Spend any time on the beach at Platys Yialos?"

"Got there one day, but mostly we hung around the town. A lot of Swedish girls were doing the island, and I was sort of occupied," Gary said, dispalying a lascivious grin.

"I lived on that beach for two weeks. I'd teamed up with this guy from the States and we bunked in at an old sheep herder's shack," Bill reminisced, as he hoisted the stubbie.

Memories shot back and forth at the speed of thought. Twenty minutes later Bill and Gary were acting like a pair of old war buddies.

"Hey Billy, I've got a box crammed full of first year notes, if they'd be of any help, then please let me know."

"Wow! Thanks, I'd love to have your study stash."

"Tell you what; drop by Jersey on Sunday night, and pick 'em up." Gary then excused himself, before wandering off to talk to a bunch of Wildlife boys who were gathered in the kitchen.

William Francis, feeling like he now had a big brother on campus, went outside to look for Eddie. Much to his surprise he found Edward H. Samson standing on the front steps, chatting up Gail and Judy.

"How long have you two been here?" Bill shouted from the porch

Judy smiled when she saw Billy. "We just arrived. Gary's car looks great. It's hard to believe it was painted by hand."

"Yeah, you can't beat a good hand job," Ed snickered.

"Eddie you're turning into a dirty old man," Gail scolded.

"He's already achieved seniorhood in that category," Bill chortled

"Very humorous Carlsen, but I think it's time we got back to those ivy covered walls." After a short round of see ya laters and we're bound for Scabville, Ed and Bill piled into the Bug and headed north.

It was four-thirty by the time they got back to campus. Having worked up an appetite from the arduous brush work, they went straight to the dinning hall.

Several bus loads of students were away for the weekend and the place was practically deserted. Bill noticed Donna Parker sitting by herself, and asked if she wanted company.

Donna gestured to the chairs beside her. "Be my guest."

"This is my friend Ed Samson."

"Pleased to meet you Ed," she said, before taking a sip of milk. "Did you guys get down to the Bear Flag?"

"Sure as shootin'," Billy enthused. "boy does Gary's car ever look nifty."

The threesome chattered away like red squirrels in a white pine tree while they ate their meal, but as soon as they'd finished Ed excused himself to call home. Bill and Donna lingered for a minute or two as they drank their tea. He'd contracted an instant case of indolent fever, and asked her if she'd care to go for a walk before returning to Udderson.

"I really should study," Donna sighed. "but what the heck, it's the weekend."

*

They ambled south on Bull Street till it crossed the Clydesdale River. Finding a footpath just past the bridge, the young couple started to stroll along the banks of the slow moving waterway. Two-hundred yards downstream, Bill noticed a secluded picnic table resting under an ancient maple. The stately tree had just begun to change its coat to autumn red. He suggested that they sit and watch the ducks paddling around at a bend in the river.

"Do you make it up to Port Carter much during the school year?"

"Only at Thanksgiving and Christmas."

"Well at least you get to see your folks once in a while. You know, maybe it's because we've crossed paths with many of the same people, or something, but I feel as if we go a long way back," Bill mused.

"I'm surprised I never met you when you worked in the Port, but I think I remember seeing you with Sandra King."

"Yeah, that was me. We went out together for a month or so."

"A summer romance eh? Do you ever hear from her Billy?"

"Naw, we broke it off when her boy friend came home."

Seeing a flicker of pain in Bill's eyes, Donna did a complete one-eighty. "What are you going to do after you get your degree?" she asked brightly.

"Well, nailing down that piece of paper will be a big challenge but if the academic Gods are kind, I'd like to give teaching a whirl."

"That's interesting, because I hope be a Home Ec. teacher someday."

Bill spontaneously reached out and grasped Donna's hand. "Hey, how about that, if by the miracle of miracles I get the sacred roll of parchment, we might wind up in the same school."

"Don't sell yourself short Billy. You're smarter than the average bear, and I'd put money on you getting a ticket. I'll bet you'll be a cracker jack teacher too."

Donna gave his hand an affectionate squeeze and Bill was encouraged enough to put his arm around the lovely Miss Parker. They sat that way for a several minutes and much to Bill's surprise, Donna rested her head on his shoulder. He decided to go for the bundle and turned her face gently towards him. Encountering no resistance, he brushed his lips over her sweet mouth. Their kisses and touches became more fervent and intimate until Donna suddenly pulled away.

"I have to catch my breath," she murmured sleepily.

"God you're beautiful," he whispered softly.

"W-We'd better get back, I-I really do have a few things to do this evening."

"You're right," he rasped, slowly shaking his head. "I should read some more *Canterbury Tales* before I go lights out."

"My God! I hated Chaucer when I was in first year."

"Well things haven't changed a bit, if it wasn't assigned work you couldn't pay me enough to read about some wife having a bath."

"That's a good one Billy," Donna chuckled happily.

33

On the hallowed steps of Udderson, he reluctantly said good-bye to Donna, then returned to his room. He hit the books as long as he could stand it. Feeling drowsy Bill put his head down on the desk for a brief rest. The next thing he knew it was well after mid-night. Slowly wiping sleepy grubs from his eyes, Billy padded over to his bed and safely tucked himself in.

6
*

Following a hearty Sunday breakfast of scrambled eggs, bacon and pancakes William Francis was ready to take on the world. Nothing was open in the city on the Sabbath except the churches, so there was no point going into town. Bill wandered out to the practice field in front of Hereford and watched the school's rugby team working out. While he was standing there, a husky, broad shouldered hooker, nursing a bruised ankle, limped over to say hello.

"You used to play high school football," the wounded warrior stated assuredly.

"H-How'd you know that?" Billy stammered, wondering if this guy was some kind of psychic.

"I was talking to Charlie Ross at the dinning hall yesterday and he pointed you out, by the way, I'm Taffy Morgan."

"Bill Carlsen, pleased to meet you."

"So would you be interested in playing rugby?"

"It looks like fun but I really can't afford the time."

"We practice once a week and play on Saturdays, our first fixture's in a fortnight, we only have five this season and they're all on weekends. ."

Shacking his head slowly, Billy stuttered self-consciously, "I-I don't have any equipment."

"No problem. The club supplies shorts, jerseys, socks and boots."

"To tell you the truth Taffy, Friday at Phys. Ed. was the first time I tried to do anything connected with rugger."

"Not to worry boyo, you can pick it up as we go along. We need a scrum-half. All you have to do is roll the ball into the scrum, curl around behind the lads, grab the ball when it pops out and pass it off to the man beside you."

"Sounds easy," Bill said.

"Now lets see, you're just about my height and weight." Taffy stroked his chin for a moment before asking, "What size of shoes do you wear?"

"Number tens."

"Well then you're in luck, because so do I. I've a spare kit in my club bag over there. Why don't you take it, change in your room, then join us on the pitch?"

Bill had nothing better to do and wanted to get some exercise. By the time he got back, Taffy had worked the soreness out of his ankle, and took Bill over to meet the rest of the team. He was given a few brief instructions, then before he knew it Billy was running with a ball that had squirted from the scrum. In a fit of panic he shoveled it to the first orange shirt heading west.

There were enough upright bodies present to form two teams of eleven-a-side, and a short scrimmage followed. When Bill got the ball he was unable to pass it off. A gigantic prop forward, who resembled a grisly bear about to pounce on a piece of raw meat, closed in for the kill. Billy took off like a frightened deer towards the end zone, figuring he could get rid of the overgrown pigskin in a few steps. Taffy must have loaned him his Ladyluck rugger boots, because after dodging several tackles and employing a well aimed straight arm he found himself on the pay dirt side of the goal posts.

*

Bill stood there totally amazed. Out of the corner of his eye, however, he was suddenly very aware of the colossus he'd avoided at mid-field rocketing towards him like a runaway locomotive. He heard Taffy yelling, "For God's sakes man, drop to the ground!"

Billy immediately crumbled to the turf a split second before the steaming freight train, that bore a striking resemblance to a rugby player, whistled to a halt. The Goliath, still huffing and puffing, reached down to help him up.

"Nice try old chap," the behemoth mumbled.

"Hell I scored. Whattaya mean nice try?"

"A try *is* a score you bloody twit."

Bill scratched the back of his head, figuring it might take a while to get the hang of this game.

After the practice Taffy invited the side back to his place for a social. Taffy was a Welshman as the story goes, but Glynn Morgan, Bill's new friend, really was from the land of Dylan Thomas. He shared a rented home in downtown Sowsbury with three other lads who played on the team.

*

"Would you take an ale?" Cecil Lewis, the hulking prop forward shouted, while hoisting a bottle in Bills direction. Bill grinned openly. "Yes please!"

"You colonials are always so formal."

"Yeah, I'm just a wild colonial boy," Bill laughed, remembering the term his grandmother had used when referring to Canadian soldiers in the Great War.

"You know, you've some bloody strange games on this side of the pond. I've watched hockey, baseball, and this thing you call football on the telly. Good Christ man, football's a sport where you use your feet, not your bloomin' hands," Cecil snorted derisively.

"You Brits have your ways and we have ours," Bill countered, the hairs on the back his neck beginning to bristle.

Spotting a glimmer of rising hostility in Bill's eyes, Cecil decided to back off."I'll drink to that Billy me lad!" he laughed heartily.

In addition to the outspoken Mr.Lewis, Taffy shared his pad with Sandy Alexander who hailed from Glasgow and Paddy Flannigan a native of Belfast. The U.K. was indeed alive and well in the Great Dominion.

*

It was a fantastic afternoon. All the beer you could drink, all the songs you could sing and all the sandwiches you could eat. Bill was in fine form when he staggered out of Taffy's basement and headed back to the College. After a weary climb up to the third at Hereford, he managed to flump down on his rack in 301 and crashed for the remainder of the daylight hours. In his afternoon dreams, Billy ran like the Greek god Mercury and scored at will.

William Francis awoke with a start at seven-thirty, suddenly recalling he was supposed to see Gary Barker before Sunday became history. Billy reluctantly arose from his bed of rest, and set out for Jersey. Bill located Gary's room without difficulty, but experienced a twinge of guilt as he tiptoed past the common room.

"How's it goin'?" Gary asked in a friendly manner, when he saw who was at the door.

"It's been a super day," Bill exhaled pleasurably, briefly filling Gary in on the rugger practice.

The sophomore President was busy with several items of year business and didn't have time to socialize. He handed Billy a tattered cardboard box full of notes before politely ushering him out of the dorm.

*

It was well past eight when he returned to Hereford. Shortly thereafter, Bill placed the treasure chest of written materials on the floor next to his desk. Pete, who was standing by the window, suggested they go down to the common room and catch a little eye. By the time they got there, Ed Sullivan was thanking his boob tube audience for tuning in to watch another, 'really big shew'. "Gunsmoke" was on next, and Billy was totally enthralled as Matt, Chester, and Kitty out smarted the guys in the black hats. When the tower clock chimed ten Pete threw in the towel. Bill agreed that he too needed to hit the sack. Yawning and stretching, they made their way to the third floor.

*

As Billy drifted off, he thought that it had been quite a week. Seven days ago he was a wet-behind-the-ears kid fresh out of high school, but now he was a bona fide student at the second biggest Cow College in the province. Just as the sandman dropped a bucket of grit on his sagging eyelids, Bill heard someone singing as they crossed the parking lot three stories below. The words of the song, carried softly on the crisp fall air, barely registering in the convoluted tunnels of Frosh Carlsen's half-awake brain.

38

On the steps of Jersey crying like hell
There is a new born babe
You oughta hear the little bastard yell
Where is his father, who can he be
Just another illegitimate child from F.U.C.

39

7

There was only one thing left that had to be resolved between the Frosh and the Sophs—an annual event known as 'The Tomato Fight'. It wasn't a contest sanctioned by the omnipotent powers at the S.A.C. It had been banned in Buffalo and also at the Cow College, but this didn't stop the student body from pursuing the time honoured tradition. The all mighty administration at Hay Seed U wisely turned a jaundiced eye to all things unofficial.

The University had its main campus, but being an agricultural school it also owned goo-gobs of acreage east, west and south of the ivory tower. It was on one of these plains of flat, rich southern Ontario farmland that the battle would occur. It, of course, had to be at night so the rulers of the Aggie Empire could be safe in their snug wee beds, completely ignorant of anything those wild and wooly under-graduates might be up to.

*

"Come on Billy we're just about there," Eddie panted, as they ran half-crouched along a winding, moonlit back forty access road.

"Hey, I can see car lights coming," Bill warned. "Head for those shrubs!"

They didn't want to be seen by the Sophs who were motoring to their section of the playing field. Bill and Eddie had volunteered to infiltrate the enemy lines and bring back any information that might be useful concerning second year tactics. They managed to stay out of sight of the Ford pickup that passed close by their hiding spot, and several minutes later reached the edge of a hedgerow where the opposition would start their attack.

"Look at that weird contraption over there," Eddie hissed, "I think it's fog machine."

"Sure, and I'm James Bond," Billy retorted softly.

"No guff Carlsen, the bad guys are going to use it for cover when they come at us."

"Well in that case Jocko Thomas we'd better report to Police Headquarters."

They double timed it back to the Frosh side of the trenches and spilled the beans.

"Okay here's the drill," Homer Sedgewick, the newly elected class President orated confidently."The Sophs are betting they won't be seen because of their smoke screen, but this is what we'll do....."

Everyone listened intently and agreed to what the leader of the pack had suggested.

*

The fog machine, a devise used to lay down a protective layer of mist over vineyards in the fall, when an early frost was forecast, puffed and snorted like a monster out of hell as it chugged inexorably towards Froshville.

The Sophs peered cautiously from behind a grey protective blanket but there was no enemy in sight. When the boys from '66 were well past the spot where the freshmen should have been, they heard whoops and blood curdling yells from behind moments before a barrage of half-rotten tomatoes came whistling at the backs of their heads.

The startled second classmen executed a rapid about-turn and began to unload their supply of red, ripe ammunition at the guerilla force attacking from the rear.

Billy caught a squishy projectile in the forehead and was blinded for a moment by the seeds and pulp that cascaded over his eyes. Most of the Frosh, however, survived the initial onslaught because they'd seen fit to liberate a secret defence system—several dozen high tech, state of the art, galvanized, solid steel garbage can lids. These circular shields, each sporting a firm U-shaped handle, provided a perfect barrier to repel the juicy hand bombs hurled in their direction.

*

Both sides gave as good as they received, and by the time the supply of love fruit had been exhausted, it was with a great deal of howling and triumphant war cries that the 'Battle of Tomato Ridge' came to a thundering halt.

41

The freshmen and sophomores approached each other cautiously at first, then amidst shouts of: "Welcome to the Cow College." the jubilant foot soldiers shook hands and patted each other on the back.

"Hey Billy, you look a little red around the gills," Gary Barker bellowed.

"Yeah, I should have bobbed when I weaved," William Francis snorted.

"Jeez Carlsen, you sure got hammered!" Eddie shouted, his voice carrying like a megaphone in the moon bright, star spattered night.

"Okay guys I get the picture," Billy chuckled, while wiping his face with a handkerchief.

"Come on you two," Gary said, while pointing towards a Ford pickup. "We've got a half-ton over there crammed full of beer, hotdogs and buns. Our treat eh?"

*

Someone had already lit a fire and they soon found themselves on the edge of a sugar bush where Coleman lanterns were being strung up on several overhanging branches. Homer Sedgewick, church key in hand, was hard at work knocking the helmets off a square of stubbies and passing around the suds as fast as his big mitts could manage. A selection of saplings were available at the edge of the woodlot and it wasn't long before a bundle of sharpened sticks were ready to impale the foot long wieners.

"Boy do these ever taste good," Billy mumbled. His mouth full of Shopsy's Ball Park specials and Jane Parker rolls.

"For sure Billy, and pass me another beer will ya?" Ed belched, while polishing off his fourth dog.

"All this Frosh and Soph stuff seems kinda stupid," Billy speculated quietly. "but I guess it's part of tradition and will go on as long as there's an S.A.C."

"Who gives a rip Carlsen, about all that philosophical crap, I've had too much fun tonight to get serious."

"Yeah, me too Eddie," Bill agreed, bending his head full back to catch the dazzling coruscation dancing above him.

42

The lids, borrowed from various trash containers dotted about the campus were returned the next day, and the fog machine found its way back to the Crop Science drive-shed. No harm had been done and the Administration, well aware of what had gone on thanks to the all powerful grapevine, emitted a collective sigh of: "Do ya mind the time?"

8

*

A Physics, Botany, Zoology, or Chemistry Lab. in the post-mortem hours, and three lectures before lunch helped to keep Clem Kadiddlehopper out of trouble, but it tended to make him one hell of a dull boy. If this weren't enough, all of the afternoon experimental sessions required a sixteen ton paper extravaganza. The sacred Laboratory Report was due, no excuses accepted, the following week. Calculus and English were the exceptions, but essays and problem sets managed to fill in those wasteful, idle moments. Phys. Ed. on Fridays just required that you show up. If you didn't drop dead of a heart attack after swimming fifty lengths, could chew gum and walk at the same time, or were still standing after wrestling a hay stacking champion from Clover County, then you were sure to get a credit.

*

By the middle of the third week the freshman were starting to wilt. Wednesday night Bill was frantically trying to put the finishing touches on a glowing dissertation, extolling the wonders of the imagery cleverly disguised in *Guliver's Travels*, when he heard a knock on his door. Pete was over at Yorkshire on a heavy study date with his new girlfriend Tova. Since the butler had taken the night off, Bill was forced to get up, from his desk of cruel and unnatural punishment, to see who was hammering outside in the hallway.

"Hey Billy how're they hanging," Eddie roared, "there's a call for you on the landline."

*

On every floor Ma Bell had unselfishly placed a one armed bandit opposite the elevator. Bill thanked Ed and hurried to the phone. He picked up the cold, black Bakelite receiver fearing the worst. Dad had totalled the car, Grandma was in the slammer on drunk walking charges, his sister Brenda had broken her arm playing volleyball, but instead he heard:

"Hi Teddy it's Kitty."

Kitty Carson was a Registered Nurse that Bill had met during the summer of '61 up in Port Carter. She was originally from Toledo, but had recently moved to Detroit and was working in the O.R. at a hospital located near the centre of Motown. They were good friends and had kept in close touch since the Muskoka days.

*

"Holy smokers, is it ever great to hear your voice."

"Yours too Billy, I got your letter last week, and decided to give you a ring."

"Is everything all right with your family?" Bill crossed his fingers, remembering that her father had major cardiac problems.

"My dad never felt better and thanks for asking. Say Teddy, I'm driving up to the Port this weekend, and I was wondering if you'd like to come along."

*

Bill hesitated for a moment realizing that he should hang around campus and hit the books, but as usually happens to most red blooded, patriotic, God fearing Canadian males, the direct circuit that runs from the brain to the hot rod, carried the day. Nice nurse Carson was a gorgeous, redhead who believed in the sanctified principals of free love.

"Beauty Kitty, what time will you pick me up?"

"I'll be there at four on Friday, if that's okay with you?"

"Perfect, my gym class ends at three-thirty. I'll meet you in front of the Hogstroff Hall. It's the aircraft carrier you'll see at dry dock once you turn off the highway."

"I've missed you Teddy," Kitty purred invitingly.

"I'll be counting the hours," he gulped noisily.

"See you soon Billy, and remember the good ship Lollipop."

When he first met Kitty, they'd punched the backword button on the time machine of their minds, recalling a mutual fascination with the Shirley Temple song, long before the Dick and Jane years. It had become an insiders farewell for them when they talked on the phone.

"Yeah, and Peppermint Cove," Bill whispered.

45

Rugby practice was held on Thursday in the twilight hours. Their first game was to be a week Saturday. The scrimmage went well, and Bill was starting to get the hang of it. The players decided to go down to the Empire after the work out, so it was another late night for the aspiring scrum-half. He missed the dreaded eight o'clock the next morning, but did manage to colour in the rest of his timetable, including the afternoon Physical Endurance contest. He arrived in front of Hogstroff at four, just in time to see a white Cadillac convertible—top up—appear on the horizon. Kitty Carson had borrowed the family chariot for the drive north.

"Teddy you look great," she burbled, as the car came to a full stop. "do you mind driving the rest of the way? I'm a little tired."

"No problem, I haven't been behind the wheel for at least a month. Playing chauffeur for a beautiful woman will be fun."

*

They motored up country chatting away like long lost cousins, until a case of the big hungeries grabbed them. Kitty wanted to stop at Paul Webers, a new burger joint on highway eleven. They ordered cheeseburgs, fries and chocolate shakes. It was getting too cool to sit at a picnic table, so they ate their food in the car.

"How's the new job going?" Bill garbled, while chewing a large chunk of meat and bun.

"My probationary period's over, and they've offered me a permanent contract."

"You must have done something right," Bill replied happily, sharing in her joyful mood.

"Yep, now they have to tell me why I'm being fired instead of booting me out the door."

Kitty was twenty-four, and had been nursing for three years. Elizabeth Catherine Carson, the name on her birth certificate, was very fond of William Francis, but had several other boyfriends. She was truly a woman of the sixties, enjoying the uninhibited lifestyle of the times.

46

Naughty, but nice nurse Carson had read somewhere that every girl should have younger lover, and the kid from the Cow College was more than happy to oblige. She drove the rest of the way to Port Carter, arriving at her parents cottage shortly before eight. It was cool inside the living room, but Bill soon had a miniature barn burner going in the ceiling high, fieldstone fireplace.

Kitty found a bottle of red wine in a wash stand by the kitchen door. She carefully removed the cork, placed two cut crystal glasses on a tarnished silver tray and joined Bill by the fire. Enjoying the comforting warmth of well seasoned birch logs, they sat on pillows and watched bright red tracers erupt from the sweet smelling wood. The rich Bordeaux was extremely mellow and awakened the taste buds with its rich blackberry finish.

"God, you look beautiful," Bill sighed estatically.

Kitty set her glass aside, let down her shimmering red hair and gently kissed him on the lips. Bill suddenly had an image of Jane Wyatt in the movie "Shangra-La" and knew how Ronald Coleman must have felt. In due time the pillows became a make shift bed and then, slowly but deliberately, in rhythm with the now flickering flames, their love making became tender and complete—camera discreetly goes of focus, and that's a wrap folks.

*

Bill awoke the next morning on the bottom bunk, of a creaky old set, in the guest bedroom. Kitty, who liked to sleep alone, was warmly entrenched in her parents big double bed. She had stated firmly that snoring and tossing bodies could spoil a good nights rest. He wasn't offended since the main event of the evening had occurred in front of the glowing, toasty marshmallow atmosphere of the large open fireplace.

The refrigerator was well stocked and Billy, up with the birds, decided it was time for the first call. He put together scrambled eggs, bacon, pancakes, hot buttered toast and a fresh pot of perked coffee.

Kitty, smelling the delicious odours wafting towards her bedroom, emerged from under the covers and joined Billy at the breakfast table.

"Good morning sweet Princess." He bowed from the waist, while a yawning nurse Carson wiped the dryness from her eyes.

"Did you get a good nights sleep Teddy?"

"The very best your Royal Highness," Bill chuckled.

"This is a great meal loyal cook Carlsen," Kitty acknowledged the title regally.

"Yeah, all that training two summers ago didn't go to waste eh?"

"Why yes, Sir William you have come a long way," she purred mischievously.

"W-What would her Ladyship like to do today?" he stammered, his temperature starting to tickle the upper reaches of the mercury.

"Well Chester," she drawled, momentarily switching characters. "since we can't stick around here till the cows come home and screw our brains out, I'd suggest that some outdoor exercise would be in order."

"By golly Miss Kitty, I'd be glad to donate my cerebral cortex to the cause of medical science if that would help."

"We are most impressed by your willingness for sacrifice deputy Teddy but me thinks that the restorative powers of the fresh Muskoka airs are more appropriate on this fine northern day."

"As you like it." Bill knelt before her, hoping he'd quoted Shakespeare correctly.

They walked to the Voyageur trial that began on the south shore of the Chippewa River, then headed east for two miles until the inland west loop was reached. Following a rugged climb up a steep, rock strewn slope they were able to enjoy three spectacular lookouts on ridges high above the wide river valley. It was a pleasantly cool, fall day. The leaves had turned, transforming the surroundings hills into a colorful quilt suspended on a giant, undulating loom.

"You know Teddy this is my favorite time of the year," Kitty sighed, as they looked down at the familiar outline of Crater Lake.

"Yeah, and no bugs to drive you bananas either."

In this part of Ontario, black flies, deer flies, moose flies and mosquitoes could make the spring and summer months a bit of a challenge. These were *not* the realities advertised in glitzy tourist brochures; featuring gleeful children at play along the shores of a secluded lake.

"That really is the best part Billy, as a matter of fact, the first addition my father put onto our cottage was a screened-in porch."

"My dad did the same thing at our North Bay camp, if we don't burn Pic up there during the summer you'd get eaten alive." Bill shivered, hearing the high pitched whine of a million bloodthirsty mosquitoes.

*

An hour later they'd reached the end of the trail and were at the edge of town. It was short walk from there to the cottage, where Kitty put together a simple lunch of mushroom soup and ham sandwiches. As soon as the kitchen was cleaned up she entered the living room. Bill was sitting on an over-stuffed sofa reading a National Geographic. Kitty sat down next to him and stated brightly, "I'd like to visit a nurse friend of mine, who lives out on Pinetree road. Do you mind spending the afternoon alone."

"No sweat, I wanna drop in at the Hilltop Café, the siren song of nostalgia and all like that there eh?"

"Okay Teddy," Kitty chuckled. "I should be back by five."

Shortly after the bumper of the Cadillac disappeared around a bend on the winding road next to the river, Bill took a slow stroll down memory lane to his former work place. The first surprise came when he went to the counter and asked how his old boss Paul Evans was doing. He was told by the waitress that Paul had sold out recently, and was now working as a chef in Toronto. This came as a shock, because Billy knew how much Paul enjoyed owning a restaurant.

49

Putting his astonishment aside, William Francis decided to order a Hires Root Beer float for old times sake, and was deep in thought when he heard, "How's it goin' Kid?"

Bill spun around quickly and sure enough Doc Livingstone, flashing a grin a big as all outdoors, was standing right in front of him.

"H-Hey Doc, is it ever great to see you," Bill stammered, as he grasped the out stretched hand.

"What are you doing in this neck of the woods Billy?"

"I'm up here with Kitty for the weekend."

"Why Billy the Kid, you sly old bandit."

It was the Doc, the town's milkman and renowned water skier, who'd pinned the Kid label on young Master Carlsen. They'd established a routine in the past and would usually slip into a wild west pipe dream.

"Golly smokes Roy, me and the little lady's just good friends," Billy whistled through his teeth—Gabby Hayes take a back seat eh?

Bill and the Doc started to talk over old-times, but soon ran out of steam. Their worlds had changed, and as hard as they tried it became awkward to keep the conversation going. *It really is true! You can't recapture the past.*

The Doc sensing the distance between them, became restless and jumped to his feet. "Got to by movin' along partner, hope to see you further on down the trail."

"Keep them silver bullets polished up," Bill muttered, trying to prolong the fast fading memories.

They shook hands slowly, neither one making eye contact. When the Hilltop's spring loaded storm door snapped shut, it silenced a brief, sweet song that Billy would never hear again. People drift in and they drift out, but we're better for their drifting.

9

*

When Kitty returned from visiting her friend she suggested that it would be nice to check out the Harb for supper. The Harbour Restaurant was the other four star establishment that Paul Evans used to own, and the place where Bill had received his training as a short-order cook. He told Kitty about Paul selling out and since she hadn't been in the Port for awhile, this was news to her as well.

*

Halfway through their meal Bill frowned thoughtfully before saying, "You know, it just dawned on me, we can't go back in time, we go back to places, but the places have changed and so have the people. I feel like a stranger in the Port now there's no one here I can really relate to." He went on to tell her about meeting the Doc and how at the end, common ground had disappeared faster than a gumboot in a wet ploughed field.

"You're right Teddy, there are times and seasons, that's just a fact of life."

"Yeah, but it makes you sorta hollow inside when memories don't match reality."

"You've been reading too many heavy duty novels," Kitty teased.

"By golly, soon I'll start taking myself seriously and always look for the hidden meaning in everything," Bill chortled, seeing a brighter side.

*

It was well after nine when they returned to the cottage. Kitty found a bottle of whiskey in her father's liquor cabinet and mixed up a couple of rye and gingers. They sipped their drinks, while sitting on a couch directly in front of the fireplace. Bill had placed several maple logs on top of a pile of cedar kindling, and the hardwood was just starting to catch. When they'd finished their Seagram's specials Kitty led Bill into the master bedroom. After slowly undressing, the sleepy pair crawled under the cool, crisp sheets.

It was a paradise found within the cacoon-like comfort of the big double bed. Kitty insisted, that this time, her Teddy bear remain beneath the soft, eider down duvet to protect and please the fair Princess, the whole night through.

*

They were on the road by ten the next morning, and decided to take a different route home. After reaching Bala, Bill set the compass for highway sixty-nine. It was an unusually warm September morning and Kitty wanted to stop for a picnic lunch. She had made several roast beef sandwiches, and packed these along with bottle of dry white wine in a wicker hamper.

A mile north of the Moon River bridge William Francis and nice Nurse Carson stopped at a Department of Highways picnic site, located on the north bank of Gibson creek. Bill got the basket from the back seat and Kitty grabbed a blanket. They discovered a trail that followed the waterway down stream and found a very private spot two-hundred yards from the parking lot. It was past Labour Day, and the area was completely deserted. Kitty spread a well worn Indian blanket on the ground, before arranging the sandwiches and wine. She'd packed two glasses and poured a liberal portion for each of them. It was a spectacular meal and the contents of the smoky green bottle rapidly disappeared.

Feeling sexy and carefree, Kitty whispered softly into his ear, "Billy, I want you to lay back on the blanket."

Not wanting to disappoint a lady he complied immediately. Taking the initiative, she led him into a world of sensual splendor that seemed to last forever. Or, if this were a Hollywood movie, the driving pistons of a steam locomotive, a piercing whistle and a clanging wig-wag would now be filling the silver screen.

*

"You drive Teddy," Kitty bubbled happily, when they finally returned to the Caddy.

"Cloud number nine express, departing on track ten!"

It had been a good one so far for the fabled CPR steam jockey 'Cannonball Carlsen', and the car radio resonated his king of the road mood when the Four Seasons began to sing, "Walk Like a Man".

The drive to Sowsbury was a downhill run all the way—light traffic and a clear, warm fall day. It was late afternoon when Billy wheeled the flagship of the General Motors fleet around to the back of Hereford Hall.

*

"It was fantastic Kitty, this is the best time I've ever had in my life." The endorphins were still coursing through his blood stream, and he was on top of the world.

"It was marvelous for me too Teddy," she cooed musically.

He gave her a long lingering good-bye kiss, then reluctantly made his way towards the dorm.

*

"How was the weekend Billy?" Pete shouted, as his roommate entered 301.

"Too short, good Aggie Eastman, but other than that, it's great to be back on campus. Anything happen while I was away?"

"Except for free beer in the milk coolers Saturday night, it was pretty dull."

"Free friggin' what, where?"

"Yeah, it kinda got me that way too. I went for the evening meal at Barf Hall and filled up my tray as usual. When I put my glass under the milk spigot a golden stream of bubbly liquid, with a head on it, came tumbling out. I was about to say something when Charlie Ross, who was right behind me, whispered, 'If you know what's good for you Frosh, sit down, offer a silent prayer to the ale Gods, and enjoy.' I did as I was told but I passed my glass off to the guy sitting across from me."

"What happened then?" Bill asked, hanging on every word.

"I ate my meal and watched the parade of astonished faces at the coolers, but no one from the dinning staff caught on because everyone was keeping their mouths shut."

Pete, who'd been sitting at his desk, got up and strolled over to the window before continuing. "When I got back to the residence I met Ed, and he filled me in. Several, yet-to-be-named ale merchants from Year sixty-four, with some inside help, had snuck into Barthman and replaced the moo with suds."

"No kiddin', and I missed it," Bill sighed disgustedly.

"Yep!" Pete crowed smugly. "It's one of those moments that'll live in Sow U folklore forever."

10

More lectures, more labs, more assignments, more essays; it never let up. Bill was starting to panic. *How in the hell will I be able to cope with this, and make a passing grade?* In order to release some air from his over inflated brain, William Francis skipped a mid-week Botany class and went to the coffee shop in the basement of Yorkshire. He was sitting by himself enjoying a hot chocolate and bran muffin when Gary Barker walked down the stairs.

"Ditching are ya Billy? Gary frowned.

"Yeah, I'm going ape-shit with all this academic stuff."

"You've gotta stick it out. The first term's a real wood choppers ball."

"Give me a break will ya? I know the party line about S.A.C and home for the Yuletide crap, but it's starting to get to me," Bill whined.

"Okay Frosh, here's a bit of free advice. Stop being a suck and get off your royal ass. Whoever said it would be easy? If you can't hack it, then stay down for the ten count and save yourself a pile of cash."

Bill blinked several times and was about to tell Mr. Barker to perch and rotate when he realized Gary was right. "Well you sure as hell didn't pretty it up."

Without saying another word, Billy opened his copy of *Major British Writers* and started to read a fascinating poem by some over-omer named Wordsworth.

*

A contrite Teddy Carlsen was on time for the last lecture of the morning and the afternoon Zoology dissection—butchering a dogfish shark was a real blast. Oh, for the fragrant aroma of formaldehyde wafting on the stagnant zephyrs of an airtight black-benched laboratory.

On the serious side, Bill had made a pact with himself to attend everything printed on his timetable, and to give it his best shot. He might still flunk out but at least he'd know, down deep inside, that he wasn't a quitter.

Billy enjoyed the rugby practice that evening and was looking forward to their first match of the season. The final round of wind sprints was followed by the usual social at the Empire, and it was well after the bewitching hour before scrum-half Carlsen finally crashed.

The next morning began with no breakfast and a couple of aspirins, but Bill was on time for his eight o'clock. By the end of the day William Francis could hardly stay awake and decided to make an early night of it. He went straight back to the dorm, after surviving another succulent repast at Barfman, and tried to do a little scabbing. Billy was about to head for the showers when Eddie poked his head through the door.

"You wanna make it to Young Peoples?" Ed grinned, a three pronged fork slung casually over his shoulder.

"Nope, it's lights out early for this kid. I had a few too many at the pub last night."

"I talked to Judy at supper. Boy, has she ever got the hots for you! She'll be there eh?"

"O-Okay, but only for one or two," Billy gulped, starting into a full colour, Vista Vision fantasy where the lovely Miss Lawson was being most cooperative.

*

It was a glorious night. Torrents of amber lager, pickled eggs and polish sausage evaporated faster than a minority government in Ottawa.

"My Gawd, these horse cocks are great," Eddie mumbled, between chunky chews on an elongated coil, while Gail and Judy were visiting the powder room.

"Why do you suppose they always go to the can together?" Billy asked, ignoring the comment about equine genitalia.

"Must be some kind of protection thing or something," Eddie coughed, before applying the flame from his Ronson to a fresh coffin nail.

"I guess it's just one of those enduring mysteries of the universe, that we mere mortals will never figure out," Bill opined, after another sip of O'Keefe's finest.

Someone must have hit the fast forward button on the time machine, because it seemed like only a moment ago they'd arrived at the L&E, and now the waiter was announcing the approach of the four wheeled pumpkin. On the way back to campus in, Ed's Bug, Bill was having a very steamy time of it in the back seat. Judy, gloriously inspired by the nectar of the Gods, had a gentle grip on the primary component of William Francis's jockey shorts. Bill, wanting to maintain balance in the cosmos, began to explore the southern regions of Miss Lawson's silk panties. They were still in this less than romantic configuration when Ed pulled into the rear parking lot of Hereford.

*

"Here's the keys Billy, just in case you wanna drive Judy over to Our Lady," Ed hiccuped softly, a moment before he and Gail stumbled out of the car.

"Goodnight my friendly," Bill modulated dreamily, recalling Mickey Lester's parting line on CKEY, 590 on your radio dial.

They both watched as Ed and Gail entered the back door of the dorm and disappeared up the stairs.

"Boy, is he ever lucky to have a room all to himself," Bill gasped, as Judy slowly unbuckled his belt.

"Yeah, but if he gets caught with Gail up there, it's curtains for him," she giggled, while Billy fumbled with her bra hooks.

"Did you bring anything with you?" Judy cooed, in between soft moans of pure delight.

He frantically rummaged around in his front pants pocket, and with a large sigh of relief extracted a foil wrapped condom.

"Aren't you the clever one," Judy purred, while tearing apart the tiny package.

The windshield was just beginning to mist over, when they were rudely hoisted back to reality by a gentle tapping on the rear window. The elf-like hammering was followed by a deep, rumbling voice, "I'll give you folks thirty seconds to make adjustments before I turn on the spotlight."

"My God, it's Trigger Taggert," Judy whispered hoarsely.

"Who in the hell's Trigger Taggert?"

"The campus cop!" she squeaked.

Displaying a series of quick change moves, they set a new land speed record for becoming presentable.

By the time Officer Taggert directed the blinding beam from his long handled flashlight into the back seat, the innocent young lovers were sitting side by side holding hands. Billy slowly opened the door and cautiously emerged into the chilled, damp air.

"Good evening Trigger, I-I mean sir. Nice night eh?" Bill cringed. *Holy doodle, I just said Trigger.*

"Well son," Taggert chuckled, knowing full well what the Aggies called him. "it's past one in the morning, and time to get the young lady home."

"I fully agree sir, and thanks for the thirty seconds."

"I was young once too you know. Get along now, and find another place to park the next time." Trigger turned off the powerful flashlight and returned to his idling cruiser.

Bill quickly wiped the cold sweat from his brow, locked up the Beetle, then walked Judy back to Udderson Hall.

*

Despite his pact and well meaning intentions, William Francis missed the Friday morning rise and shiner. He ran into Ed at lunch and felt a little less guilty because lover boy Samson hadn't been to any of his classes.

"Jeez Eddie, that was some night!" Bill yawned, before thumping onto a hard metal chair opposite his drinking buddy.

"Tell me about it Carlsen, between the sausages and pickled eggs I've produced enough natural gas to heat the entire city of Sowsbury. Now I know how a balloon feels."

"I wouldn't light up for a day or two if I were you Eddie."

"Gawd you're such a hambone, so did you score with Judy or what?"

"Naw, I never got the chance, Trigger Taggert busted things up just as I was heading for home plate."

"Yeah, I've heard about the long arm of the law here at Sow U."

"Hey, its just about time for Phys. Ed. We don't want to be late for a class that's named after you huh?" Eddie rolled his eyes, ignoring Billy's feeble attempt to become the next Jack Parr.

11

Sunday was a cool, rainy day, perfect conditions for a fixture according to Taffy, who knew all there was to know about the noble art of rugger. The University of Toronto Varsity Blues were in town and the rugby Woodchucks were pumped. All went well until the opening whistle. Strictly speaking and from a sportsman's point of view, Cecil Lewis concluded after the game, "It was bleedin' poor form for the boys from the Queen City to deny the chaps from the home side an opportunity to handle the ball." Perhaps the headline on the sports page of the local rag said it all: *Hogtown 54 Upchuckers 7. Well done lads!*

*

The irony of the whole thing was that Bill managed the only try of the day for the old orange and yellow. A Varsity player, who they later found out was colour blind, mistook William Francis for a blue and white jersey and passed him the ball. Billy, much to his surprise, had a clear path to the goal line and wasted nary a moment looking a gift horse.

The social afterwards was anything but doom and gloom. The boys from 'Toronto the Good' were all invited and the assembled mob had a roaring time.

*

"Jeez whiz Taffy, this is so unlike football," Billy thundered, in order to be heard over the raucous crowd in the cellar.

"Why yes, we try our best to murder each other on the pitch, but afterwards we usually come down by here and have some fun. Quite unlike your colonial sports."

"Yeah, if this were hockey or lacrosse we'd hate the other players guts until we could get even. It's the Canadian way."

"A keen observation boyo, some of the fist-a-cuffs that you see on the Telly make you believe in that line: I went to a fight the other night and a hockey game broke out."

"Do you like hockey?" Bill chuckled, remembering the brawls he'd witnessed at the Georgetown arena.

"Most friday nights, in the winter, I'm in attendance at Guernsey Gardens to watch the Bulls play." The Sowsbury Senior A team had several players with NHL experience and their games were always entertaining.

"Hey, that sounds like a real blast and Gary Barker told me our College squad will be pretty good this year."

"Yes, the lads have been improving," Taffy agreed.

"Well Taff, I thank you once again for the beers and cheers, but I'd better get back and do some serious grinding. Have a good one eh?" Billy waved over his shoulder, as he hurried up the stairs and out the back door.

The rugger party had ended the weekend on an upstroke, and Bill was set for another thrilling week at the Cow College. There really were cattle on campus. The S.A.C. had a large Animal Husbandry department and the beef barns were located across from the Biology building. On the Vet side, a wide variety of creatures great and small were always front and centre. Seeing the various critters was one of the neat things about attending the Porky Pig Institute of Higher Confusion, as the locals called it.

*

By early October things were starting to become routine. Bill still cut the odd class, but he was getting most of his assignments in on time, and gold stars were plastered all over his forehead for never missing a Lab. He'd seen Judy several times since the Trigger incident and was becoming very fond of her. Kitty had called him the week following their trip to Port Carter, and hinted at another visit sometime after Thanksgiving. His love life was humming along nicely.

*

The evening of October the third started off very quietly, but at eight-thirty Ed banged on the door and things changed abruptly. "It's a panty raid!"

"Holy moly, who thought this one up?" Billy gasped, jumping to his feet.

"Sixty-four, but everyone's invited."

61

"Count me out," Pete protested vigorously. "if Tova knew I was there, she'd nail my knackers to the outhouse door."

They were taken aback by Pete's direct speech. Normally if his arm were deep in beaver doo-doo he wouldn't say boo. William Francis, however, was willing to try anything that might rescue him from the clutches of Joe W. Grind.

It took them two minutes to reach the sidewalk in front of Udderson.

"A-Are you going in there Eddie?" Bill stammered, hesitating by the steps of Our Lady of Perfect Pastries.

"Yep, this'll be a night to remember, and anyone who doesn't pick up a pair of panties is a pansy," Ed yelled, taking two steps at a time.

Billy, not to be out done, followed several other berserk Aggies, and barreled into the wild silk yonder.

Once through the massive doors he was surprised to see a group of F.U.C. lovelies shouting encouragement to the unruly bunch who stormed the staircase to the upper floors. The young ladies of impeccable virtue were enjoying things as much as the stampeding herd of noble knights all high on testosterone overload. Billy stayed behind a wedge of half crazed Vets until they reached the second floor. Teddy Carlsen, the aspiring panty snatcher, came to a dead stop when he spotted Judy standing by an open door.

"What in the hell are you doing here?" Bill shouted, before remembering where he was.

"Waiting for you lover boy," Judy purred seductively, while handing him a pair of lacy, black panties.

"Well, how about that! Now, which way's the fire escape?" he puffed nervously.

"Down there," Judy told him, while pointing towards the end of the darkened hallway.

William Francis hit the metal fire stairs on the run, and descended to ground level at the speed of sound. Billy then walked slowly to the front of Udderson and was amazed to see hundreds of Aggies and Vets cheering, like they'd won the Stanley Cup.

He picked Ed out of the crowd and went over to compare notes. Ed was grinning ear to ear, as he pulled a flaming red brassiere out of his back pocket.

"W-Where did you get that?" Bill gulped audibly.

"Well, it ain't from Simpsons," Ed snorted, "I was halfway down the first floor hallway when a blonde bombshell handed me these grapefruit holders, and they were still warm."

"You'd almost think the girls were expecting the raid."

"A truck load are pinned to Seniors, so I don't think they'd stump the panel on "I've Got a Secret."

"Being pinned to someone must really hurt eh?" Bill deadpanned.

"Oh Cisco!" Eddie showboated, slapping Billy on the back.

"Oh Pancho!" Bill chortled.

The Cisco Kid and his sidekick Pancho were riding the range once again—a snowy Saturday morning image, on a round-screened ten inch Admiral.

*

All the Aggies and Vets who were going ashore had already been there, and things were beginning to settle down when a staggering Charlie Ross, flying higher than a Sputnik, bellowed, "Let's hang 'em from the flagpole."

The charging student body, resembled a buffalo stampede as it rumbled its way towards the towering metal pipe opposite the school's artillery piece. The halyard was rolled down, then four score and ten items of the most intimate feminine attire were attached by hockey tape to the tightly twisted wire.

The raucous honour guard, gathered around the upright standard, solemnly saluted as various bits of nylon, elastic and lace were hoisted skyward. Ed in the meantime had been talking to a bunch of year sixty-seven classmates. He had somehow managed to assemble a ball of waxed string, a roll of electrical tape and a handful of panties and bras. He gave Bill the follow me sign and disappeared into the inky darkness. The excitement had died down and the 'Raiders of the Lost Drawers' were beginning to disperse.

Billy, his curiosity fully aroused, tagged along to see what Eddie was going to do. When they were out of sight of the maddening crowd Eddie said, "Trigger and the campus grounds crew will have those flags down within the hour, but I don't think anyone will check the water tower."

"You've got to be out of your tree Samson to even think of climbing up there at night."

"Hell, I'm not afraid of heights, and if I pull this off it'll be a perfect ending to the big raid."

"Yeah, but if you don't, it'll be the perfect ending to you," Bill cautioned.

"Don't get your toga in a knot Carlsen. I just want you to act as my lookout again."

"Okay, but remember, I faint at the sight of blood and brains scattered all over the sidewalk."

"Very funny Billy, but I've climbed the tower at home a hundred times, so easy does it."

"All right Eddie, I guess someone's gotta watch out for you."

There was a mercury-vapour standard at the bottom of the water tower, and a band of red strobes at tank level. Bill melted into the shadows while Ed began his upward journey. It seemed like an eternity, but by Billy's watch only twenty minutes had elapsed when Eddie stepped onto terra firma.

"Lets get back to the dorm, like yesterday," Bill pleaded.

"My God, do the lights of the city ever look great from up there," Eddie rasped.

After reaching the third floor, 'high wire' Samson whooped, "Boy, could I ever use an ale."

"Sounds great to me, but just one eh?" Young Master Carlsen was starting to fade.

The barley sandwich slid down like a raw oyster on a half shell, and it was with good reason that Billy began to yawn and stretch. It had been a big day. With eyelids at half-mast, he wished Eddie a bundle of erotic dreams, then retired to the peace and quiet of his room. William Francis crawled in and went fast asleep.

The next morning, bang on Eddie's prediction, the flagpole had been stripped clean and was flying the Canadian Ensign. The water tower, however, was the focal point for all students on campus, and it wasn't until high noon that the fire department erased the lingerie show from the front page.

*

There are winners and losers in every event. The Sowsbury President, in his infinite wisdom, concluded that all male students of both Colleges were likely involved, one way or another. He therefore fined each and every ball bearing Vet and Aggie ten dollars. This tickle money, as some of the Frosh called it, was to be added to the next terms fees—*tough titty said the kitty when the milk ran dry.* He also informed the fair maidens of Udderson that the University would reimburse them for any losses.

The F.U.C. beauties, all being shrewd Home Ec. types, put their collective heads together and calculated that ten times twelve hundred red blooded specimens of young Canadian manhood equalled a very large bunch of Queen Elizabeth's portraits printed on one dollar bills. The four-hundred inmates of Our Lady submitted a bill for thirty dollars each.

"These broads will sure as hell be able to figure out a family budget," Charlie Ross grouched, when he discussed the incident with Billy several days later.

The upside of the underwear for cash trade was realized by various and assorted Vets and Aggies who were privileged enough to see their girlfriends decked out in some of the finest frillies this side of heaven. In addition, the all powerful grapevine had revealed that Eddie was the one who'd climbed the tower to hang the washing out to dry. From that point on, Edward H. Samson became a walking, talking legend at Moo U.

12

*

The homecoming football game was played on 'Raid Day' plus two. The Woodchucks were winless to date, but figured the cheering alumni would help them carry the day. However, they were up against the league leading Western Mustangs and it didn't look too promising for the old orange and yellow.

Billy had asked Judy to go with him to watch the big match. She accepted readily and suggested that a dram or two of liquid refreshment, containing a dash of spirits, might be in order. William Francis, wanting to satisfy Miss Lawson's desire for a beverage laced with a splash of Kickapoo joy juice, purchased a mickey of Silk Tassel at the Sowsbury liquor store. Pete's ID came to the rescue once again when the manager asked Billy for 'proof of age'.

Before the game he topped up a half-filled 12 ounce Wilson's Ginger Ale bottle with rye, then carefully hammered the crown cap back into place. Bill placed the bottle into a small paper grocery bag and was now ready for a short stroll over to Udderson.

*

It was a glorious, warm October day. Crumpled Kleenex clouds paraded serenely across a robin's egg sky—a metrological display that gave promise to a prolonged Indian Summer. The good folks of Sowsbury were a little nervous, claiming they'd pay for this easy fall come February.

Billy arrived at the girls residence on the stroke of one, and waited patiently for Judy to emerge from the inner sanctum. Miss Lawson resembled a picture right out of a Hollywood movie magazine when she finally descended the steps to ground zero.

"Boy! Do you ever look sharp" Bill marvelled, trying hard not to drool at the sight of his girlfriend dressed in tight fitting black slacks and a well filled out white blouse. He handed Judy the bottle and nodded appreciatively when she stuffed it into her purse.

Ten minutes later, they entered the bleacher side of the gridiron, and scrounged around for two fifty-cent pieces, before being admitted to the high rent district. You could sit on the grass opposite the stands for free, but Billy had shifted into another one of his movie fantasies. He was now Humphery Bogart, a gold plated kingpin, escorting a gorgeous dame to the best table in the house.

*

Trigger Taggert was on duty looking for students trying to smuggle booze into the stadium, but observing nothing suspicious he waved Judy and Billy on by. They soon found two prime seats, ten rows up, on the forty yard line.

*

It was just about half-time and the Mustangs were ahead by a touchdown. William Francis having acquired a severe case of the big thirsties croaked, "I think it's time for a drink."

"Me too Billy," Judy replied, while reaching for her purse. She'd barely moved a finger when they heard a muffled explosion—*carbon dioxide gas expands when heated eh?*

Several seconds later, golden droplets of a sweet aromatic liquid began to ooze out of her black leather hand bag. Bill did the only sensible thing. He quickly grabbed the purse, and tried desperately to catch the outflow in his wide open mouth, holding true to the Carlsen family motto:"*Waste not want not.*"

Billy suddenly realized that people in the stands were staring at him and managed one last surreptitious lick before handing the soggy bag back to Judy.

*

Meanwhile, back at the ranch, the Chuckers had recovered a fumble on the Western twenty-five. Charlie Ross scooped up the pigskin with his massive right hand and steamrolled into the end zone. The crowd went wild. The convert was good and the game was tied. The entire student body, except for the Vets, broke out into the Aggies fight song—a cacophonous chorus that could've be heard in Ottawa.

67

You're a hardy fellow old orange and yellow
We'll pull for you today
We'll fight all night for the College on the heights
And hear her song till our dying day
So bash right through we'll root for you
Old Aggies never die
The Vets waiting for their chance yelled: **They just smell that way!!**
We'll cheer, cheer, cheer for the College
And lift her banners to the sky.

It was the pinnacle of the homecoming festivities, and Charlie was everyone's hero. The unbridled euphoria continued with a thunderous rendition of the Sowsbury victory cry.

Orange and yellow
Oh so mellow
On to Victory
Chuckers, Chuckers
Bronco buckers
Tougher than a bee

  The poor sports from London apparently didn't like the singing or cheering. They hogged the ball for the entire second half and scored thirty unanswered points.
*
When the game finally ended Billy and Judy walked dejectedly back to Udderson. Part way to the residence he remembered there was still half a mickey of the hard stuff in 301. William Francis told Judy about the stash in the dorm, then barreled up the stairs to the third floor and retrieved his prize.
  "There's a quite spot behind the football field where we could sit and talk," Judy said, when Bill returned with the liquid treasure hidden in his briefcase.
  "Sounds like a plan to me Jude."

An old growth woodlot bordered the southern side of the football field and was indeed a very private place. A shimmering canopy of iridescent golds, reds and burnt orange, hovered above the young couple as they sat on a blow-down log deep in the heart of Sherwood Forest.

*

Bill took a snort, then passed the whiskey bottle to Judy. "Sorry I don't have any mix."

"No problem, my dad likes to drink his rye neat and so do I," Judy replied, before hoisting the glass turkey.

"Yeah, but it burns all the way down," Bill gasped audibly.

"After your eyes stop watering it's rather pleasant," she rasped, following a king sized belt of Mr. Walker's snake oil.

"You know, I can hardly believe it, I've been here at the S.A.C. for over a month now," Bill whispered hoarsely, the roaring blaze in his throat beginning to subside.

"This is my second year and I'm just amazed as you are," Judy sighed, moving towards him till their shoulders were touching. "I wonder what the future will bring?"

"Why think of the future or the past? Let's just be content with the here and now."

"That sounds a little too simple Billy. We'd always be denying where we've been and where we're going."

"Hell no! We gotta confine our lives to day capsules," he protested loudly.

"What's a day caspool? I-I mean capsule," Judy stammered, after another shot of Hiram's hooch.

"It's the twenty-four hour sphere you travel in. Your life's enclosed in a magic time bubble, and nothing from the past or future can bug you."

"Sounds kinda weird to me," she laughed uneasily, looking at Billy as if he were several stubbies short of a square.

"Well Jude, it's simply a thought, composed of nothing but smoke and feathers," he assured her, seeing the look of concern in her eyes. "I guess we'd better make tracks before my bubble bursts eh?"

Judy intoned softly, "Billy, you're a real card."

They walked slowly, hand-in-hand, towards the edge of the enchanted forest. There was a faint whiff of burning brush on the gentle westerly breezes and a subtle hint of dry, decaying leaves scenting the late afternoon air. Their world was peaceful and serene, much like President Kennedy's Camelot, where it only rained at night, wizards were good guys, and dogs never pooped on the palace floor.

13

The Rugger match on Sunday turned out to be a red letter day for the lads. They beat Western handily and restored a modicum of honour to the battered pride of Sow U. The side now had a one and one record and the basement socials went from good to gooder. The grinning Welshman was indeed a happy hooker. Whenever Taffy was kidded about the position he played, the response was always the same, "Any resemblance between me and a lady of questionable ethics is purely coincidental."

*

The following week was uneventful and Bill left the campus right after his Friday Phys. Ed. class to hitch home for the Thanksgiving weekend. He was decked out in his brand new Aggie jacket and got a ride from the third car that came by. The driver had just come from Fulford and was going as far as Langston. He let Bill off two hours later, half way along the Main Street of Georgetown. It took him another ten minutes to walk to his parent's house.

*

The Carlsen's residence was an early fifties two-story home that has been built in a quite subdivision located on the edge of town. There were open fields at the back of the house and Holstein milkers still grazed beside the page wire fence that separated the tiny town lots from rolling pasture land to the south.

He opened the front door and was greeted by his sleepy-eyed father. Bill's Dad worked for Trans-Canada Airlines and was currently on the graveyard shift.

"Hey, it's the College man! How are you Son?" his father beamed, as they joyfully shook hands.

"Just great Pop. Is Mom home yet?" He'd barely got the words out when Barbara Carlsen hurried down the stairs.

After a big hug from his mother, she carefully inspected him at arms length and declared, "You look awfully thin Billy. Do they feed you enough, up there at the College?"

"The food isn't exactly restaurant quality Mom, but there's plenty of it. I've been playing Rugby and I guess I've run off a pound or two."

Bill's grandmother who'd been down in the rec-room watching her favorite soap, came up the stairs when she heard voices. "Sonny, It's so good to see you," she burbled, while wrapping her arms around him. "have you been eating properly young man?"

"Relax Grandma, you and Mom must be in cahoots. We get three chow calls a day at the dinning hall. It's not like home cooking, but it's better than anything I could put together."

While Mrs. Carlsen and Granny McNair applied the finishing touches to supper, Bill followed his dad out to the garage. Harold Carlsen carefully popped the hood on the Chevy Biscayne, then standing shoulder to shoulder, father and son contemplated the endless mysteries of the internal combustion engine.

"She's been running a little rough lately. I think it might be the timing. If you could hand me the strobe light Billy, we'll check her out."

They worked—a friendly silence between them—on the family chariot for forty-five minutes, then returned to the kitchen. Bill's sixteen year old sister Brenda had arrived home while they were playing mechanic. She let out a large squeal, preparatory to a rocket launch into Bill's outstretched arms. "Gosh, you've lost weight. Don't they feed you when you go away to College?"

His father snorted happily, "It's unanimous, all the women in this house think you need to be fattened up. I hope you arrived with a healthy appetite."

The pot roast was delicious and Bill gladly accepted a second helping. To cap things off he had a big plate of bread and gravy, after the meat was finished. He still had a hollow spot and devoured a large slice of lemon meringue pie for desert. Twelve thousand Calories later Billy waddled into the kitchen to phone his best friend Dave Graham. They'd been pals all the way through high school.

Billy, however, hadn't heard from Dave since they went their separate ways in the fall. Dave was enrolled at Ryerson in the Business Administration option. Following several short rings, Dave's father answered the phone. After the usual pleasantries were exchanged, Bill's number one buddy came on the landline.

"How's it goin' Slick?"

"Like gangbusters Tex," Bill chuckled, feeling good to be using their old nicknames. "so do you wanna get together tomorrow night or somethin'?'

"I'd love to Billy, but I've met this far out snuggy, and she's invited me to her place Saturday night for supper."

"No sweat eh? I just wanted to say hello."

The two friends talked away for ten minutes before his mother shot him a look that could only be interpreted as: "What if an important call was coming our way?"

"My mom wants me to get off the phone just in case the Queen gives us a ring," Bill sighed noisily. He could hear Dave chortling at the other end. Tex fully understood, because his own mother did the same thing whenever a telephone conversation lasted more than the time required to hard boil an egg.

"Sunday we're going up to my grandparents place in Owen Sound, so Monday's it Billy."

"I guess were toast. Dad's still on midnights, and I've got to be back on campus for a rugger practice. We'll get together over the Christmas holidays," Bill replied dismally.

"Take care Slick. See ya real soon."

"Sure thing Tex."

Feeling like a stranger lost in a familiar place, he realized the parade was passing on by. Life changes, people change, but don't you wish that some things could go on forever.

Saturday night Bill and his dad watched "Hockey Night In Canada". It was one of the first games of the season, but the Leafs were looking good. Bill Hewitt called his usual competent game, and Peter Puck was the his usual cute pain in the ass.

73

"I think they're good for another cup again this year,"Mr. Carlsen affirmed, when the game ended two zip in favour of the boys from Carlton Street. Johnny Bower had recorded his first shutout, and Frank Mahovlich had scored both goals for the Toronto Maple Leafs. The Juliette Show was next and shortly after 'Our Pet' wished her TV audience a goodnight, Billy headed for his upstairs bedroom.

*

The Carlsens had their Thanksgiving turkey on Sunday. Granny McNair out did herself and everyone overdosed on white meat, dark meat, stuffing, cranberry sauce, mashed potatoes, green peas and gravy. The pumpkin pie with whipped-cream for desert turned out to be the crowning touch.

Bill was up early Monday morning, and caught the Grey Coach bus for Sowsbury at nine. He walked back to the campus from the station, played quick change artist in the dorm, and was on the pitch by two. Taffy, as expected, invited the squad back to his place when the practice was over. God ruled the heavens, and the galaxy pulsated peacefully in its swirling journey through space.

14

Mid-terms were but a week away and the pressure cooker was starting to whistle. Bill, feeling the strain, did the only sensible thing; he called Judy and invited her to Young Peoples. They had a great time complaining about all the studying they still had to do. It was getting towards midnight when he popped the question.

"Would you like take in the picture show Saturday night? *Viva Las Vegas* is playing."

"I'd love to Billy!" Judy smiled promisingly, after a large slurp of Carling's Black Label—official drink of the gods, and fruit of the hop flower.

Ed was home grinding and had loaned Bill his wheels. When the pub closed William Francis, several spinnakers to the windward, drove carefully back to the campus but managed to run the Volks up over the curb in front of Udderson. He was now parked on the lawn, a worms length from the steps that led upwards to the pink splendor of Babeland.

"Gee thanks Billy, now I won't have to walk very far," Judy giggled." See you at the movies."

He watched her until she was safely inside, then clunked back over the curb and drove slowly towards Hereford. Bill missed the dreaded eight o'clock the next morning, but did manage to fill in the rest of his dance card.

*

Pete had his overnight bag packed Friday afternoon and told Bill to have a terrific weekend. He was heading home to the big smoke for some of Mom's apple pie. As soon as Pete closed the door it crossed Billy's devious mind that he was now home alone, and all things were possible.

The Saturday fixture was a romp over McMaster. The side was jubilant, and now had a winning record. This was all well and good, but no one really gave a rat's ass about Rugby. The win at homecoming by the lads was ancient history. Football was the only sport that mattered, even though the gridiron Woodchucks hadn't won a game all season.

After the match, Bill attended the social, but left early in order to put on the feedbag before his heavy date. Billy thought the source of the beef stew might have been a dozen or so old leather shoes, but he did manage to chew the overdone chunks of mature cowhide into small enough pieces that he didn't choke to death. Following the restorative powers of the three S's, he left Hereford and strolled over to Udderson.

Judy wanted to walk uptown but Billy insisted they take the bus, and not be late for the first show. "I hate coming in part way through a movie, then having to stay until someone says; holy Toledo isn't this where we came in?" Bill orated, as they waited patiently in the public transit shelter.

The picture was a typical Elvis spectacular—lots of glitter and a multitude of forgettable songs. Judy thought that Ann-Margret looked like a bimbo. Bill, however, valiantly pursued his Miss Margret fantasies till the flick ended.

It was a beautiful mid-October night. There was a bite to the air and a hint of smoking leaves that tickled the nose like a milkweed parachute. Bill and Judy held hands as they walked slowly back to the College. After reaching the steps of Our Lady of Perfect Pastries he smiled winningly. "Pete's away for the weekend, and I was kinda wondering, if you'd like a guided tour of our third floor penthouse?"

"As in come up and see my etchings," Judy chuckled.

"Y-Yeah, something like that," Bill sputtered.

"God, if we get caught by your Proctor, you'll be in big trouble," Judy warned.

Each floor in the residence had a student who acted as a house mother, or in this case father. It was the Proctor's job to make sure that the rules were enforced. No babes and no booze, being two of the biggies.

"Harry Guardwell's our floor fink but he's way over at the other side of the third." Bill squeezed her hand reassuringly. "My room's just three doors from the top of the staircase."

"Well, okay," Judy hesitated. "I'll go as far as the parking lot but it we see anyone, I'm history,"

When they arrived at the landing that led to the third floor hallway, Judy stayed put while Bill scoped things out. Since the coast was crystal clear, he left the door partway open before reporting back. Three seconds later, they were safely within the cosy confines of 301.

"See Jude, that was easy eh?" Bill exhaled slowly.

"Easy?" My heart's still going a mile a minute," Judy gasped, as she plunked herself down on Bill's bed.

They undressed hurriedly in ragged stages, ultimately finding puppy-like pleasure in the wonder of their naked bodies. There was no Trigger on duty to interrupt things this time.

Bill shuddered slightly, when they came up for air. "You're the most beautiful girl on campus."

"I was sure wrong about the Teddy bit when we first met at the pub, King of the beasts suits you better," Judy growled softly, pleased by the compliment.

The happy couple talked and laughed for an hour, thoroughly enjoying their private world. Judy looked at the clock on Pete's desk and was surprised to see that it was well past the bewitching hour.

"I'd better be getting back," she yawned sleepily.

"Okay Jude, but I've gotta tell ya, this is the best night I've ever had," Bill sighed pleasurably.

The young lovers made it safely to the landing of the third floor and were starting down the stairs when Harry Guardwell suddenly appeared on the way up to his room.

"O-Oh hi Harry," Bill chirped. "I-I'd like you to meet my sister Brenda, she's here for the weekend and I wanted to show her my room."

Billy had two fingers crossed behind his back and Judy was silently uttering a continuous stream of Hail Mary's, hoping the Proctor wouldn't recognize her. Harry, the floor fink, looked at Judy suspiciously before unloading, "For Christ sake Carlsen when it says no girls it means family too. I oughta report you to Dean Angus, but if this really is your sister, he'd probably let it go."

"Jeez Harry, I'd really appreciate it if you'd forget about this terminal brain cramp."

"Okay Carlsen, you and your sister, or whoever, better get the hell out of here, and in the immortal words of Douglas MacArthur, never return."

Judy was the first to speak when they emerged into the frosty, early morning air. "That was a close call. I think Harry recognized me, but he was really being a good guy."

"Yep, Guardwell the top floor screw just went up one-hundred percent in my books," Bill said, stifling a yawn. "The next time I'm by the In and Out I'll pick up a school boy for our guardian Proctor."

Several minutes later they stepped into the deking bushes in front of the residence, in order to say a proper goodnight.

"It's been fantastic Jude. I wish it could last forever."

"That's a beautiful thought Billy but with mid-terms and all, we should be heading for Scabville."

"Yeah, I've got to do some heavy duty oil burning like yesterday, time to play fairy godmother and turn into a pumpkin."

"You know sometimes I need a translator to even know what you're talking about."

Bill grinned. "It's all part of my Frosh mystique and besides, I've been studying Shakespeare and he's pretty deep."

"Billy, you'd make a great artsy-fartsy type. You should transfer to Queens or some place like that."

"Nah, the Cow College is where it's at. God you look gorgeous in this light."

They kissed , smooched, necked, and groped for another ten minutes. Parting is such sweet sorrow as Christopher Plummer once said, but then again, it was time for all good boys and girls to enter their separate kingdoms.

"You're the greatest Jude," he murmured softy, as the lovely Miss Lawson let go of his hand. She was too sleepy to reply, but nodded appreciatively before ascending the golden staircase that led to the hallowed sanctuary of virginal repose.

15

*

It wasn't very glamorous, but potato salad kept Billy from flunking out of College. The Sunday dinner at Barthman was cold cuts, crusty rolls, coleslaw and spud salad. It was a great meal and William Francis thoroughly enjoyed it. He tried his best after supper to scab for the Calculus mid-term but reading Tolstoy in living Russian would have made more sense. The hidden messages buried in Sir Isaac Newtons invention remained undiscovered. As it stood, he didn't have a banana tree's chance in Yellowknife of passing the test.

*

Bill struggled to keep his eyes open, but before the clock struck twelve he was fast asleep—head glued to the desk. Pete was pissed at Billy for staying up so late, however, forgiveness illuminated his ever Christian soul when he heard gentle snores coming from across the room. Several sighs later, good Aggie Eastman rolled over and began to count a succession of lovely, bare breasted maidens jumping over a low cedar rail fence.

*

At the first hint of daylight Bill awoke with a case of gut cramps that had him doubled over as he raced for the bathroom at the end of the hall. An hour later, instead of starting the Calculus exam, he was fastened to the throne hoping the end would come soon. When things finally settled down William Francis gingerly walked over to Hogstroff and asked to see the campus nurse.

*

Billy was perspiring heavily when he went into the examining room with Miss Hancock. He didn't know if he was going to be sick to his stomach, or have to make a mad dash for the facilities.

"You're the tenth this morning," Hanna Hancock clucked sympathetically. "When did it start?"

"Just about the crack of dawn ma'am. It hit me like a sledgehammer."

She took his pulse, blood pressure and temperature, before handing him an evil smelling, oily, dark liquid to drink. R.N. Hancock then gave Bill a stoppered bottle full of runny, pink, chalky stuff and said he was to take two tablespoons of the disgusting concoction every three hours. He was also given very firm orders to stay in bed all day.

Resting peacefully on the rack was impossible, because half the time he was chained to the white telephone. His toilet companion, *The Study of Plants: A Science*, wasn't as entertaining as *Lady Chatterley's Lover* but it did help him to prepare for the Botany brain twister the next day.

Billy made the rest of his scheduled tests and was granted a medical excuse for missing Calculus. When the results came back he'd passed everything but Physics and had an average of fifty nine percent. The Administration couldn't force you to quit after the mid-terms, but they advised anyone with two or more flunk bombs, and less than sixty percent, that chances of passing were remote. The staphylococcus bacteria, that bloomed like a rose in Bill's potato salad Sunday night, had kept him from a second failure and receiving a cheery suggestion from the ruling chiefs to take a hike.

*

Since his marks were low and he'd failed one course, Billy was placed on the Dean's endangered species list and ordered to report to the head Aggie for counselling.

The Dean of the S.A.C. was Doctor Abraham Angus. He had a PH.D in Soil Science. The Dirt Department was a big player at the College. Bill bumped into Charlie Ross at Barthman, the day before his interview with Abra-Dean Angus, and pumped him for information.

"What's he like?" Bill asked the big senior.

Charlie furrowed his brow for a moment before paying the old Dirt Doc one of the highest compliments an Aggie could bestow. "Old Abe's a real good shit. When I was in first year, somehow a two-four wandered into my room, and was discovered by our floor fink."

"When I got hauled up on the carpet in front of Doc Angus," Charlie continued." he asked me if the beer was mine. I wasn't going to lie and I told him that, yes it was, but he was welcome to have one with me anytime he wanted to."

"What did he do then?"

"He let out a big laugh and said that at least I was honest and had a sense of humour. He let me off with a warning and that was it."

The next day Bill went to see Dr.Angus at four o'clock. He was sent directly into the Dean's office as soon as he arrived. The great man immediately rose to his feet, skirted the large mahogany desk and shook Bill's hand.

"I've seen you play rugby Carlsen, it's nice to know that one of our teams is having a winning season."

"Th-Thank you sir," Bill rasped nervously. "we've been lucky to win a close one or two."

"Relax young man I'm here to help you. Now, what can we do to get you over the sixty with no failures?"

"It's my fault, I've been having a pretty good time and skipped a lot of lectures."

"Well, if you promise not to tell anyone, I had the same problem. I just about flunked out and would have too, if it weren't for a high mark in Soils. That was still on the Frosh curriculum in those days. I guess that's why I eventually went into the field."

"My lips are sealed sir, and boy, does that ever make me feel better about things. I'm going to give it my best shot between now and the Christmas holidays, and besides I'd be letting my great-great Aunt Ethel down if I didn't get my ass in gear."

"Who's this great-great Aunt?"

"It's a long story sir and I'm sure you wouldn't be interested."

"Let me be the judge of that Mr. Carlsen."

"Okay, but I'll try to keep it short. You see I'm here because ancient Aunt Ethel McNair left a pile of cash when she kicked the bucket, I-I mean passed away."

"Bill, I may be the Dean but I'm still an old Aggie, so tell it anyway you want."

"Thanks sir. Just before the war, when Aunt Ethel went toes up, a large portion of her estate was placed into an educational trust."

"Why didn't your Aunt leave it to her children?"

"She never married sir, and I was told by her niece Edith Graham, who's the family trustee, that Ethel was quite a lady."

"In what ways?" Dean Angus asked, a real look of interest in his eyes.

"Aunt Ethel was one of the first women PH.D.'s in Canada, and the President of a College in Pennsylvania. To top it all off, she spent her summers teaching native children how to read and write at the Grenfell Mission schools in Labrador and Newfoundland."

"That is impressive Bill, and I understand why you're under the gun. Being here on that Trust's a big responsibility."

"Yes sir, and more than anything that's what scares the hell out of me. I'm worried sick that I'll disappoint her."

"Even if you don't succeed, as long as you've done your best it'll be okay, but on the practical side Mr. Carlsen, remember your Profs. are there for tutorials if you need them."

"Yeah I know, but it's the third period and those damned Canadiens have just scored another goal."

"I can sure relate to that one, I'm a Leaf fan too. Look Bill, please don't let me or Aunt Ethel down. It's time to get off the pot and scab like a bugger between now and the Christmas Exams."

The head Aggie had forgotten himself for a moment and in someways felt like a Frosh again. Maybe that was the joy of working with young people. You took at lot longer to grow old. Dr. Abra-Dean Angus, the grey haired Dirt Doc, shook Billy's hand and wished him luck.

82

*

16

The food infection, a wayward angel in disguise, rescued Bill from the stake but a further saving grace was state of the art, high-tech. William Francis had purchased a brand new Hughes-Owens slide rule. The accompanying programmed manual taught you page by page how to use the bamboo wonder. By mid-November Billy had become proficient enough to do the calculations required for his Physics homework and Labs. In all modesty, he had to give a big assist to Eddie, a bona fide rule wiz.

"You know what? This makes problems almost fun," Bill said to the Wiz, who'd helped his apprentice with a car load of brain teasers that brought to life the wonders of the Doppler Effect. It was a cool, November's evening and the first snow of the season covered the parking lot below 301.

"Yeah, it beats the crap out of long hand," chief guru Samson blustered. "these zingers would take forever using a pencil, paper and tables for square roots and logs."

"At one time I thought logs were for burning in the old Franklin," Bill chortled. "but now that I've been granted the keys to the cosmos, they've taken on a whole new meaning."

"Look Carlsen, if you're playing Lou Costello again, I'm heading for the pit," Ed snorted, while slapping Billy playfully on the back."what say we call it quits, tomorrow the weekend begins and happy times are here again."

"Thanks for your help Eddie. Yeah, T.G.I.F. twenty-four hours from now I'll be digging into a big piece of Mom's chocolate cake."

They would be homeward bound after Phys. Ed. Their lives had taken on a comfortable routine, a long, winding road stretching four years into the distance.

*

The next afternoon halfway through circuit training the head jock, Dr. Ken Armstrong, looking like a lost puppy, slowly crossed the gymnasium floor and stated that classes had been canceled.

He then hit them with a bombshell that Billy would remember for the rest of his life, "Gentlemen, please pay attention because I have an important announcement to make," fighting back tears Armstrong rasped, "the President of the United States has just been assassinated."

All you could hear was a jet-like drone from the ventilation fans. Everyone was afraid to breathe. The chief gum chewer, unable to utter another word, executed a rapid about-face, clutching a well worn clipboard tightly against his chest as if it were a bullet proof shield.

When Bill and Eddie finally got to the dressing room a group of students were clustered around a radio that had been placed on the window ledge in the instructors office. The local Sowsbury station was carrying an American feed of Walter Cronkite informing the world that President John Fitzgerald Kennedy had been pronounced dead. It was one p.m. eastern standard time, Friday November the twenty-second, nineteen-hundred and sixty-three. A day when anyone alive in Canada, who fully understood what was going on, would be able to tell you where they were and what they were doing.

On the way to the residence Ed and Bill walked in silence immersed in their private thoughts.

"Holy smoke Billy, someone just killed the most powerful man in the world. God knows who's next," Eddie exploded, unable to hold things in any longer.

"It's a wide awake nightmare," Billy choked out the words. "We think we're going to be here tomorrow, but this sure smartens you up."

Ed shrugged helplessly. "The magic's gone and Camelot got breached. Jeesh, one minute we're snuggled in a warm fuzzy blanket, and then a total wipe out."

Pete had already taken off when Bill got back to 301. He tossed several essentials into his overnight bag, then headed out the door. He'd decided to thumb his way home instead of taking the bus. Eddie had offered to drive him, but Billy gratefully delclined—it would mean a two hour detour for Ed.

William Francis didn't have to wait long. The Aggie jacket was like a ticket, and he got a ride right away. The man who picked him up was in a daze. He first started talking about the assassination, then as if he'd completely forgotten about it, rambled on complaining loudly that the price of gasoline would soon hit forty cents a gallon. Bill hitched another ride just east of Sandberg and was home by five-thirty. An inch of fresh snow coated the front lawn of his families' house and the arctic whisper of an early winter hovered in the air.

*

His grandmother, who was preparing supper in the kitchen, carefully put her apron aside and walked towards him, arms outstretched. For some reason Bill began to cry.

"Sorry Gram, you're going to think I'm a big suck, but I feel like a little kid who got lost on his first venture around the block."

"There, there Billy. I felt the same way when your grandfather went off to the Great War."

"God, that must have been terrible," Bill snuffled, beginning to regain his composure. "Grandpa served in the Second War too. Boy, you've sure been through a lot in your lifetime."

"Why yes Sonny, but today was a shock to me as well. From what I've seen on the TV, this President Kennedy was a knight in shinning armor."

"Yeah, he stood up to the Russians, and just when it seemed that things were hunky-dory, poof you're a pile of ashes."

Bill heard a car pull into the driveway. He went to the living room window and saw his dad get out of the family Chevy—lunch pail tucked under his arm. Bill greeted his father at the front door and they shook hands solemnly, like two old friends meeting at a funeral.

"Some news eh Son? You know, I may be way out in left field, but I've a gut feeling the Commies are behind this."

"I wouldn't be surprised Pop, I figured some day Kruschev would get even for those Cuban missiles."

"If the Yanks can prove that, it'll mean war, and it won't be anything like the second either when I was a soldier, the atomic bomb has changed everything."

Father and son continued to discuss the sobering events of the day as they walked towards the kitchen. Bill's mother and his sister Brenda arrived at six. Shortly after that the family sat down for supper.

All the talk at the table was about the assassination until Mr. Carlsen cleared his throat and declared, "Well, what's done is done, and all the words we're filling the air with won't change it one single bit."

"You're absolutely right dear," Barbara Carlsen agreed. "Now Billy, how are things going at College?"

Bill threw his mother a car salesmen's grin, hoping that no one would ask him about midterms. "The rugby season's over Mom, and I'm hitting the books pretty hard, Christmas exams are just around the corner, so it's Scab City for me."

Brenda sourpussed. "You're like from Grossville Billy. Can't you college types find a better word for studying other than scabbing?"

"Sorry Sis, it's just a bit of Cow U slang," Bill chuckled. "Someday when you're old enough, I'll tell you all about deking bushes." Despite the tragic events of the past twenty-four hours, he was starting to feel secure in the safety net that surrounds home and family.

Late that evening, they learned that a man named Lee Harvey Oswald had been arrested at a movie theatre in Dallas, and was being held as a suspect in the Kennedy shooting.

"I'll betcha Oswald's a Commie agent," Harold Carlsen muttered ruefully, before heading upstairs to the master bedroom.

*

Ten the next morning was the first hint of a new day for William Francis. One eye open and the other still demanding sleep, he peeked out from under the covers, his rumbly stomach telling him it was time for the last call to breakfast.

"Hey, what's to eat Gram? "Bill yawned openly, trying to get the sleepy grubs out of his eyes. "I'm so hungry, I could munch on a groundhog's toe-nails."

"Well Sonny," his grandmother chortled, "I don't think that'll do you much good. My iron's working if waffles, maple syrup and bacon are still your favorite."

"Holy smokers, I've died and gone to a better place as Mr. Dickens once said."

"I don't think Charles Dickens ever used those words, but you being a College boy, I'll just have to assume you're right."

*

"Boy this is the best meal ever Grandma," Bill mumbled between king sized bites "we never get grub like this at Barfman."

"Where in the devil's that? Is there no decent place you can eat at that school you're attending?"

"I'm just joking Gram," Bill replied reassuringly. "they feed us pretty good up there at the S.A.C."

"Sonny, you still look awfully thin," she said sounding concerned. "Would you like seconds? The iron's still hot."

"If I eat anymore, you could stick me with a pin and I'd burst," Bill groaned, contentedly patting his bulging stomach.

Granny McNair started to laugh, realizing her grandson had just used one of her favorite sayings. "Lord love us Billy, you've learned some bad ones from this old lady."

"Gee wilikers Gram, from where I sit you're still a good looking chick. I bet you turn a head or two when you walk to the grocery store."

"My God, with a line like that the young girls will be falling all over you."

*

Bill had a second cup of perked coffee, before calling Dave Graham. He got him on the second ring.

"It's like a phantasmigorical nightmare Slick, they just iced the most powerful man on the face of the planet." Tex's voice was raw with emotion. "Mom and Dad are in Ottawa visiting friends and I haven't had a chance to talk to them."

Dave heaved a ragged sigh before continuing, "I'm kinda rattled by this whole thing, so how's about coming over and we'll have a couple of beers."

"Take it Easy Tex, it's not Armageddon. A man was killed in Dallas, but life goes on," Bill sputtered, trying hard to quell his own fears. "What time do you want me to be at your place?"

"Wait a minute Billy, my parents just pulled into the driveway. I'll call you back when I know what's going on."

Bill paced the floor for five long minutes. until the phone finally jangled in the wall cradle. "So what's the scoop?"

"Is that you Teddy?" A familiar voice asked.

"K-Kitty, holy cow!" Bill stammered. " Are you okay?"

"Not really, but I'm managing," she whispered.

"I can sure understand with J.F.K. and all. How'd you know I was home?"

"I phoned the College and someone on your floor told me you were in Georgetown. I know that my timing's rotten considering what happened to the President, but I have some news of my own and I wanted to tell you right away."

Bill held his breath figuring that the next thing he'd hear was the "P" word and one William Francis was about to face the business end of a shotgun.

"I'm getting married Billy," Kitty stated calmly. "I met an intern here at the hospital just after I got back from Port Carter and we're engaged."

Bill was torn between laughter and tears. He was sad and relieved within the passing of a millisecond, but he finally recovered enough to speak.

"Well how about that, you'll be able to play doctor and nurse for the rest of your life," Bill joked. "Seriously Kitty, I'm sincerely pleased for you and Dr. Kildare."

"His name's Bert West and Ben Casey he's not," she chuckled. "Bert wants to be a G.P. when he finishes here and practice in California. Hollywood, I'm on my way!"

"Kitty, I'll always remember you, and thank my lucky stars for the times we had."

Billy managed to exorcise a large lump in his throat before croaking, "You're the best, and remember the good ship now and again."

"Teddy I love you! Don't ever change." There was a faint click at the end of the line followed by a tunnel-like silence.

Dave Graham called back several minutes later to explain what had happened. He said his parents were really worried, so they came home early and we're now in the kitchen having a cup of tea. He had the car and was off to see his new girlfriend. She'd just called, and was in a panic. Bill suddenly felt very lonely. He kicked around the house the rest of the day, then watched "Hockey Night in Canada" with his father that evening. The Leafs looked good, and seemed to be a shoe-in for another Cup.

*

Bill was up early Sunday morning and caught the noon bus back to Sowsbury. He hit the books after arriving at the dorm, and was thinking about a slow stroll over to Barthman when Ed Samson burst into his room. "Billy, you won't believe this but Oswald just got shot. H-He was being moved to another jail and right there on TV, a guy in a black hat gunned him down. It's like out of *Alice's Adventures In Wonderland*, things are getting curiouser and curiouser."

*

The following week was filled with images of the Ruby shooting, Lyndon Johnson taking the oath of office aboard Air Force One, the far away look in Jacqueline Kennedy's eyes as the former Vice-President raised his right hand, the gun carriage carrying the body of J.F.K. to Arlington Cemetery, and John-John saluting the flag draped casket.

89

17

Within days life had returned to normal, and the hottest topic on campus was the price of draught beer. The greedy suds merchants were now charging fifteen cents instead of one thin dime for an eight ounce glass. A rebellious cry was sounded in the Sow U Sentinel for all red blooded Aggies, Vets, and Home Ecers—which rhymes with wreckers as any long faced S.A.C. Romeo would moan after a bust up with one of Flora's frails—to boycott the Empress in order to bring the hotel owners to their knees. This turned out to be as useless as weeds in a wheat field. Young Peoples was more popular than ever and the barley sandwiches flowed free.

*

"It's kinda like throwing a pebble into a big mud puddle, the ripples rush out from the centre, but before you can get your finger out they're gone," Ed grumbled, while holding a full beer glass up to the light. "Life's a dirtbag."

"That's a crock," Bill countered. "kids are being born, lovers are getting married and the Leafs are going to win the Stanley cup."

"For Chrish shakes Carlsen, doesn't it mean anything to you? We just lost the greatest man in the world?" Eddie slurred. "Where have all the flowers gone is all I wanna know?"

"Hey Samson, lighten up, it's time to mosey on over to the L&E and check out the dollies." Bill pointed in the general direction of Skirt City. "I'll bet some of the hottest babes, inhabiting Mother Earth, are awaiting our attention."

*

Shortly after entering the Ladies and Escorts side, with Edward the gloomer and doomer in tow, Billy spotted Donna Parker sitting with another girl. He tried his best to navigate a straight line towards their table. Coming to an abrupt halt two inches from a gleaming aluminum chair leg and playing the noble knight of yester-year, he executed a perfect bow.

"Lady Parker of Port Carter, I presume," Bill burped accidently, "whoops, excuse me."

William Francis swayed like a tall tree in a wind storm but managed to maintain his balance. "I see the outrageous price of Dow's finest hasn't slowed you down."

"Billy you're corned," Donna chided gently."but what the heck, we're all alone. Why don't you and Eddie sit down."

Ed and Bill descended like two turkey vultures on a deer carcass, trying their best to assume a posture of instant sobriety.

"This is my friend Alice," Donna said, motioning across the table. "she's sixty-five as well."

"Boy, what a coincidence my mother's name's Alice," Ed piped up, stretching the truth till it fractured. "so when's the contest?"

"What in heavens name are you talking about?" the blonde, blue eyed, built like a brick shirthouse Alice asked. "There's nothing happening on campus this weekend."

"I'm talking about the Miss Canada Beauty Pageant," Ed charmed, his sticky tones dripping with the sweetness of Bee-Hive Golden Corn Syrup. "You two gorgeous creatures are obviously contestants."

The girls giggled, while Bill's mind projected a sparkling image of the buxom Miss Alice, hand in hand with lover boy Samson, climbing up the back staircase of Hereford.

                              *

Fifteen cent draught was still looked upon as a stand and deliver operation, but after several rounds the foursome began to mellow, and continued to lap up the effrovescent brew until the last call sounded.

"By golly Miss Molly," Bill crooned way off key. "it's four o'clock, the movies over, and we fell asleep at the bar."

"My God, the Everly's and Little Richard would have a bird," Donna giggled. "Hey, it's after midnight and Alice is driving me back to Udderson, she has her own place and doesn't live on campus."

"Are you a plutocrat or something?" Ed smirked, using one of the ten dollar words he'd just learned in English 101. "You sure as hell look like a normal person."

Without warning Alice burst into tears. She tried her best to speak between sobs but couldn't, so Donna tried to explain.

"Alice's Mother and Father were killed in a car accident two years ago," Donna's voice cracked, then getting a grip are emotions she continued. "She lives with her grandparents."

Ed placed his right arm around Alice, before saying," Gosh I'm sorry, if I'd known I woulda kept my big mouth shut."

Alice had a vise-like grip on Ed's hand and sniffled, "It's not your fault. I just get a little carried away now and again. Look, my dad was fond of saying that life's for the living, so why don't we all go back to my place."

"We wouldn't want to disturb your grandma and grandpa," Bill interjected." It really is getting late."

"They're in Florida for the winter, and I have the house all to myself, "Alice infomed the boys enticingly, having fully recovered from her pity party."Grandpa left a case of Red Cap in the root cellar, so we won't go dry."

*

Pins dropped very quitely all over the universe as the boys contemplated the infinite possibilities before them. Ed was the first one able to speak, "We'd be glad to drop by and see your digs."

"Then it's settled. Why don't you follow us back to my pad?" Alice purred. "It's not far from here."

*

Once outside the Empress, the F.U.C. lovelies climbed into a brand new sixty-three Thunderbird. The two Aggies stood mouths agape, as they watched the girls pull away. Green with envy the S.A.C. neophytes tumbled into the bedraggled Beetle.

Several minutes later Ed brought the Bug to a full stop in front of a large ranch style bungalow located smack-dab in the middle of a Sowsbury snoothood.

With the boldness that comes from a skin full of lager, the two freshmen approached the portals of paradise. Billy rang the doorbell feeling more like the fly than the spider.

"Well walk right in and sit right down." Alice beckoned like the Sirens of old. "Would you care for a beer, or maybe some grass?"

Bill had a run in with the weed up in the Muskokas, but wasn't sure he'd heard right, and politely asked for an ale.

"D-Do you mean grass as in grass-grass?" Ed stammered.

"Yep," Donna stated knowingly. "we've got some of the best Mary Jane this side of Winnipeg."

"If you're game?" Alice challenged, "I'll build us a joint."

"Relax Eddie it's better than beer," Donna soft-soaped.

"Tell me about it, I smoked up on our senior class trip to Ottawa last spring and it was out of sight."

*

Alice disappeared into the kitchen and returned several minutes later with a sausage sized roll your own. She lit the homebrew reefer, then took a long pull before handing it to Donna. Bill was next in line and sucked in a mega cloud of Acapulco Gold. All went well until he started to choke. The stuff lit up his lungs like a blow torch, and he couldn't stop coughing. His eyes began to water, and an inexorable merry-go-round began to push him about the room.

"Easy does it Billy," Alice echoed in a far away voice. "What we have here is a first cousin to Maui Wowie."

Bill hung in until Alice got out a roach clip, then passed.

"This stuff isn't all that strong," Bill mumbled as he began to trip. He drifted along slightly above everyone's heads, hearing the others, but too involved with the pattern on the rose and carnation wallpaper to join in the conversation.

Time became a meaningless dimension within the borders of his mind, then without warning all supports collapsed as he crashed headlong into the rock face of reality, a rush of stormy seas pounding in his ears. William Francis stared at Donna with glazed eyes and heard her whisper, "You've been looking at that wall forever, you're really ripped."

Bill couldn't move his lips to speak and began to freak. Donna seeing the look of terror in his eyes, soothed gently, "Breath normally, calm down, and talk to me."

93

He concentrated on her face with all his might, then managed to rasp, "Boy was that ever strange. It was like being on another planet, but right here all at the same time." Bill slowly looked around the room and was startled to see they were alone. "Who vaporized Eddie and Alice?"

"They've gone to look at Alice's collection of dolls, she keeps them in her bedroom," Donna chortled softly.

Bill knew the only doll that would hold Ed's attention, and other locations, was the stand up Barbie who lived in Grandpa's house.

"Why don't we check out the rec-room?" Donna purred. "There's a real nice fireplace down there, and we could toast marshmallows or something."

*

Someone had already laid kindling, small logs and crumpled newspaper in the soot blackened, wrought iron basket of a red brick fireplace. Bill lit a match, then threw it on top of the tinder dry mixture. Ten minutes later, the pulsating glow of fairy-like flames had turned the cold dark hearth into a tropical sunrise.

"God, I could look at those sparkles for hours," Bill sighed rapturously. "This must have been what cavemen watched instead of TV."

"That's far out Billy," Donna cooed, as she softly caressed the inside of his thigh. "It's really too warm for this satin blouse."

She teasingly pulled the garment over her head and handed it to Bill. The sight of Donna almost wearing a lacey, black bra was a breath altering sight.

I'll bet she scored that ebony bolder holder from her fair share of the panty raid loot. What the hell, I'm about to get my monies worth.

Donna then removed her tight fitting skirt. The bone wrenching vision of jet black panties, garter belt and nylons was a feast for the horny and mighty. He couldn't help but think that old Abra-Dean-Angus really knew what he was doing when he laid on the saw buck underwear tax.

Billy fumbled with Donna's bra hooks for what seemed like an hour of watching Lawrence Welk reruns. Just before he tossed in the towel, something let go, and one of the sweetest, matched pairs, this side of the Pearly Gates, popped into his trembling hands. Flesh on flesh carried the day and soon the room was shimmering with the slow, sensual act of love.

Maybe it was the influence of the weed, but Bill experienced the most incredible sensations as they performed a modified version of the hokey pokey. The build up was a endless journey followed by a rocket launch that would have impressed the hell out of an Apollo astronaut. During the coming down phase, of their most excellent adventure, Donna murmured softly, "Boy, all that exercise has given me an appetite, let's check out the fridge upstairs."

Upon entering the kitchen, they were surprised to find Eddie and Alice sitting on the floor, devouring a tankerload of maple walnut ice-cream. Donna opened the freezer compartment of the Kelvenator and took out a tub of Borden's finest. She filled two soup bowls with the frozen nectar and handed one to Bill. The four pot heads laughed, giggled, and belched as they happily crammed a gallon of maple walnut into their over loaded tummies. Just as the first streaks of light began to brighten the eastern sky, Eddie and Bill wished the girls sweet dreams, thanked them for a bang up time, then walked slowly to the Bug.

*

They were unable to answer the bell for their lectures, but did manage to make the afternoon Zoo lab.

"So much for my vow to never miss another class," Billy bemoaned guiltily at the end of the day. He was feeling like a spaced out cadet—a vision of the "Space Patrol" gang misting across his jellybean brain. What do you suppose old Buzz Corey and Happy are doing today?

Jeez, if you can remember that Saturday morning, snowy, black and whiter, pulsating through the ether towards a well used pair of rabbit ears, you're older than dirt.

95

18

It was a Thursday afternoon, and Ed and Bill were listening intently to the Orgies Lab. Demonstrator. The Demi was a Piled Higher and Deeper hopeful whose assigned duties included the care and feeding of the freshman chemistry class.

"The ethyl alcohol you'll be using today in the synthesis of ethyl acetate has been mixed with a deadly poison to render it unfit for human consumption." Pausing for effect, the garlic breathed, armpit sniffer, whined threateningly, "Drinking this stuff will cause you to go blind."

*

"That's right from Guffville," Ed snickered, before they started the experiment. "I checked out the procedure in the library, and it won't work unless you use pure joy juice."

Eddie was the resident Wiz Kid, and had received a mark of ninety-eight on his mid-term. This was a remarkable achievement considering his spotty attendance record. Ed was blessed with a photographic memory, and loved the subject enough to have read and memorized the entire Organic Chemistry text. Billy had no doubt, whatsoever, as to the validity of his lab. partners research.

"This is the same stuff that's in rye whiskey, right? If what you're saying's gospel, we could mix it with ginger ale and have a gangbusters cocktail."

"Eureka!" Ed stage whispered. "That's why we're going to liberate some of this white lightning."

"Hold the phone Samson, if we get caught then it's curtains for me. I'm already on the Dean's hit list."

"Don't worry Billy, it'll be a piece of cake."

Eddie quickly checked the area. Confident that no one was watching, he poured the absolute alcohol from a beaker into a plastic wash bottle, then stashed the contraband in his briefcase. William Francis figured, in for nickel in for a dime, and carefully placed a glass stoppered reagent bottle, full of 200 proof, into his club bag.

The experiment was over, and the brazen booze boosters were about to leave when the Demi stopped them at the door

"That was a great lab. sir," Bill squeaked, his heart pounding like a jack hammer. "Did we do everything okay?"

"No problem Mr. Carlsen." The disheveled Doctorate candidate smiled."I'm a Rugby fan, and that try you scored in the Toronto game sure was an egg breaker."

"Thank you sir," Bill exhaled raggedly, edging slowly towards the hallway. "It was pure horseshoes."

*

Bill ran into Donna Friday morning at the coffee shop, and ordered for the both of them. Balancing two steaming mugs of fresh perked and a couple of bran muffins on a tray, he guided her towards an empty table.

"Can you make it to the party at Alice's place tomorrow night?" Donna asked, as soon as they sat down. "It'll be the last bash before the Christmas exams."

"Is Eddie invited? He's kinda stuck on Alice."

"You must be a mind reader Billy, when she mentioned the party I was given firm instructions to invite the two of you. Edward H. Samson made quite an impression in Wonderland."

Eight-thirty Saturday evening the Wiz, with Teddy Carlsen at his side, knocked three times on Alice's front door. They were greeted by Donna, who informed them that the hostess with mostess was still cloistered in her dressing chambers. She then ushered the two wide-eyed Frosh into the living room to meet the party hardy crowd.

Ed and Bill were carrying brown paper grocery bags, and when asked by one of the guests about the mysterious contents Ed stated confidently,"The magic elixirs contained within are guaranteed to make the best fruit punch you've ever tasted."

"Okay boys," Donna crooked her finger. "follow me."

One minute later, they removed two peanut butter jars, each half-filled with a clear, colourless liquid, and carefully placed them on the breakfast nook table.

Alice, who'd finally gotten her duds together, entered the kitchen. Ed explained the game plan then asked her for a large container. She went straight to grandma's china cabinet and returned with a huge punch bowl.

"Will this do?" Alice asked, holding up the sparkling, cut crystal vessel.

"Perfect!" Billy nodded, as he began to unscrew the lids on the Jiffy jars.

They mixed a jug of orange juice with a quart of grapefruit juice, then added two cans of peaches. Three bottles of Canada Dry ginger ale and sixteen ounces of, ninety-nine and forty-four over one hundred percent, pure alcohol—just like Ivory soap—completed the potent brew. Ed dumped in two trays of ice cubes from the fridge, and the punch with a crunch was ready for human consumption.

"Don't tell anyone about our secret recipe," Ed warned. "This mixture should add a little spice to the proceedings."

"Our lips are sealed," Alice promised.

Bill carried the enormous bowl into the dinning room then placed it on top of a buffet table. Donna followed with a tray full of glasses and a crystal ladle. Most of the girls at the party weren't heavy drinkers, but the idea of a fruit punch had an instant appeal. It tasted great! The combination of delicious ingredients masked the sharpness of the alcohol, and the heavenly ambrosia disappeared faster than a deer at a cougar convention.

*

"Boy is it ever warm in here," Sally Goodhead shouted, after her third glass of the wondrous nectar. She was a friend of Donna's and normally quite shy. Sally suddenly stood up and started to gyrate to David Rose's "The Stripper" booming on Alice's Hi-Fi. The pickled Puritan slowly removed her sweater, followed by her bra and skirt. Long tall Sally was about to take off her panties when Donna grabbed the wannabe Gypsy Rose and guided her into one of the bedrooms. The guys booed Donna loudly and the girls all thought that Sally could stand to lose a pound or two.

"Ho-Holy cow," Bill stuttered, his mouth agape. "this stuff's rocket fuel. I never thought I'd see a strip-tease anywhere but the Lux theatre."

When things finally settled down, someone put on a forty-five of "Hey Paula" and several couples got up to dance slow and close. The boxing glove special had been a hit so far.

Without warning the front door blew open and a pint sized hurricane, wearing an Aggie jacket, burst into the foyer howling at the top his lungs, "It's Howdy Doody time!"

The rosy cheeked leprechaun who'd just landed in Wonderland was one Howard Dewie. When Howie Dewie arrived in sixty-two for his freshmen year, he soon became known as Howdy Doody. Howdy lived in a three bedroom apartment on Bovine Boulevard, and had two roommates. This is where the story gets kind of weird. One of his roomies, Robert Cooper, hailed from Buffalo New York. Since Bob was sharing digs with Howdy everyone started to call him Buffalo Bob. The third man staring in this tall-tale-but-true was Rolly St. Clair from Chapleau in Northern Ontario. *Yep, you just hit the nail—Clarabell.*

*

The triumphant trio led by his Howdyship parachuted into the party one, two, three. The boys from Boul. Bovine had become legends in their own minds and were accepted by most of the students at Sow U as campus superstars.

"What time is it Peanut Gallery?" Buffalo Bob roared.

The assembled party animals erupted in unison. "It's Howdy Doody time!"

Believe it or not Mr. Ripley, the educated elite of the Province, and future leaders of the fair Dominion broke into a stirring rendition of Howdy's theme song. When the last sour note had all but curdled the air, Clarabell launched into his act. There was always someone new at any party and Rolly St. Clair went into overdrive for the benefit of people like Bill and Ed who were seeing the self-made clown for the first time.

"I was born in Chapleau eh?" Rolly began, with a hint of a very charming French Canadian accent. "This object I wear around my neck is not some clown's toy as I'm sure you would agree."

He paused for effect and held up a conical shaped structure constructed of very thick birch bark.

"This genuine, hand made moose horn fashioned by *mon granpère* Guy St. Clair was handed down to me by *mon père* Jean St. Clair. Now the cow moose, if she's in an amorous way, will call longingly to the bull moose. In the fall when we hunt around Chapleau, we try to imitate the call of the cow to draw a bull into the open for a shot."

One of the peanut gallery, who was in on the game, asked in very sincere voice, "Could you let us hear that call Clarabell?"

"*Mais oui, mon ami.*"

*

Ed and Bill, completely enthralled by the goings on, were bent forward anticipating a display of ancestral skills. Rolly slowly brought the authentic birch bark moose horn up to his lips and took a very deep breath. The next thing they heard was a squeaky mouse-like creature crying, "Here Moosie, Moosie."

"Gotcha!" Howdy whooped.

"Big time!" Buffalo Bob crowed.

The peanut gallery broke into a torrent of hysterical laughter, while Eddie and Bill tried to wipe the egg splatters off their crimson faces.

*

Buffalo Bob, assuming his roll as master of ceremonies, took charge and started into a well practiced routine.

"In this corner ladies and gentlemen we have the male O-rang-O-tang."

"What's an O-rang-O-tang?" the peanut gallery yelled.

"This ladies and gentlemen is a rare and amazing animal, who's been endowed with two brass balls."

"Wow!!!" the crowd whooshed.

"Right you are folks. When this incredible beast swings through the trees high above the forest floor an ear splitting sound echoes throughout the jungle, O-rang-O-tang, O-rang-O tang...."
After a small burst of canned laughter, the gallery erupted into song:

"We're off to see the wild west show.
The elephants and the kangaroos.
As long as we're together.
No matter what the weather.
We're off to see the wild west show."

Howdy had been sipping on the two-sixer of scotch he always carried, Buffalo Bob had been nibbling on his fifth of Jack Daniels and Clarabell had been taste testing his mickey of Canadian club. No pain, lots of gain, would pretty much describe the state of the escapees from Howdyville.

Howie, who'd been to Alice's place before, wandered out to the rear cedar deck and proceeded to turn on a spotlight that illuminated the entire yard. The house was built on a ravine lot that backed on to a large tract of parkland. Meanwhile, Bob and Rolly walked out the front door, headed directly for Howies fifty-eight Edsel, opened the trunk and grabbed a double barreled Cooey shotgun. They stuffed their pockets with shells before scooping up a dozen clay pigeons and a hand thrower. Clarabell, followed by his sidekick Buffalo Bob, quietly strolled into the backyard, went to the edge of the ravine, which was lit up like a midway, and started to blast away at the clay birds launched by Howdy.

Several minutes later an Aggie, who didn't smoke and was trying to catch a breath of fresh air at the front of the house, did a double take when he looked down the street and spotted a speeding bubble gum machine. Panic striken, he scrambled up the porch steps to warn Alice. She immediately doused the yard light, then quickly informed everyone about the impending arrival of Sowsbury's finest.

101

"You play the guitar, don't you Billy?" Donna shouted, while handing him a twelve string. "Okay folks let's make it look like a night at the Hootenanny."

Catching on to the game, Billy started immediately into, "Kisses Sweeter Than Wine", and the subdued peanut gallery all joined in. By the time Alice answered the knock on the front door, the peaceful scene in the living room resembled a meeting of the Mickey Mouse Club, without the silly hats.

"Cut out that racket!" A burly policeman growled, while performing a "Stompin' Tom" act across the polished oak floor. "Gunshots coming from this property were reported to headquarters."

"Gee, we never heard a thing officer," Alice cooed, as she batted her baby blues. "but you're welcome to go outside and check if you'd like."

The police made a thorough search of the property, but found nothing. Howie, Bob and Rolly, figuring that something was wrong, had disappeared down the dark slopes of the ravine as soon as the lights went out. An hour later they sneaked back to the Edsel, said goodnight to Alice, and got the hell out of Dodge.

Bill and Eddie made it a point during the party not to drink any of the punch they'd put together. However, rooting around in grandpa's liquor cabinet the two Frosh discovered three, forty ounce bottles of Logana, a fortified, berry wine from British Columbia. The dark purple nectar was delicious. William Francis and his partner in crime polished off two of the three—no point in being greedy.

Shortly after the S.W.A.T. team departed Wonderland the punch concocters, experiencing a terminal case of the big fatigues, bid their fond farewells and drove, very carefully, back to Hereford.

The next morning Bill awoke with a head two sizes larger, but definitely no smarter. *The fruit of the vine may be what you'd drink at a fancy restaurant, but right now I'm more grateful for a bottle of aspirin than that hopped up bingo from the Okanagan.*

19

Sunday morning coming down, William Francis just about tripped over Judy Lawson as she came out of Barthman. Unable to avoid her, he stopped to say hello.

"Where on earth have you been Billy?" Judy frowned. "I really need to talk to you."

Oh, oh Bill thought, here comes the wrath of a female scorned. "You know Jude, you look like a million bucks."

"Teddy, I've something to confess," Judy tittered, looking like a sinner searching for a booth. "Yesterday I received a letter from my old boyfriend back home. He mailed me his school ring and we're going steady again."

Sure enough when Bill looked at the fourth finger of Judy's left hand he spotted an imitation blood red ruby, set in a band of five-and-dime silver. *Betcha that turns green in a week.*

"I'll really miss you," Bill croaked, fingers crossed behind his back. "We've had some special moments together."

Watching soaps like "Search for Tomorrow and "The Guiding Light" with his grandmother during elementary school days had prepared him well for moments like these. *Thank God I won't have to tell her about Donna, I really couldn't handle that on my berry baked brain.*

"You're such a sweetheart Billy!" Judy gushed. "I hope we can still be friends."

"Sure thing Jude, and happy trails to you." *Well, that was laying it on a little thick but Roy and Dale would be pleased.*

He gave her a quick peck on the cheek, then headed for 301. The reality of the Christmas examinations was a dark cloud on the horizon and young Master Carlsen hadn't quite figured out what to do.

*

During the last week before exams afternoon labs were cancelled. This gave students an opportunity to study, or get assistance from a Professor. Bill, however, wasn't able to take advantage of the tutorials being offered.

He was so far behind, he didn't even know what questions to ask. A pesky bacteria had saved him from being sent down river before, but hopes of a second miracle would only happen if Mr. Chips were to open a help-line in the Yellow Pages. As fate would have it, an engraving of a caribou kept him in College. Billy took a quarter from his pocket and blurted out loud, "If it comes up heads I'm going to join the Royal Canadian Air Force, but if it comes up tails I'll study as hard as I can."

The coin flipped end over end, then rattled around several times before coming to rest on the tile floor. He peeked through half-closed eyes, and much like the diffuse beam of a searchlight on a foggy night a reasonable facsimile of an antlered critter slowly penetrated the film on the outer edges of his blurred vision —a well worn image of Her Royal Majesty face down. Bill had a sudden inspiration and looked through his closet for the box that Gary Barker had loaned him. Gary's lecture notes were all nicely organized in three ring binders and very easy to read. *Nose to the grindstone, shoulder to the wheel. Rotsa Ruck eh?*

*

Billy scabbed his little heart out during the last week of the term. He crammed all weekend, but was barely prepared for Physics Monday morning. Each exam he wrote was a three hour meat grinder. Wednesday was a real killer because he sat for Botany in the morning and English in the afternoon. By the time the Orgies brain teaser rolled around, Billy was on the ropes. It involved a lot of memory work, so he pulled an all-nighter. He did his best, but when the papers were collected, there was no joy in Mudville. William Francis was one sad, sorry puppy as he walked, head down, back to Hereford.

Enter Satchmo wailing:

Got them low down,
On the ground,
Cow College Blues.

The next day an exhausted William Francis, barely able to stay awake at the side of the road, dangled a weary thumb aloft in hopes of getting a ride as far as Georgetown. He arrived home three hours later and was greeted by his mother who'd just set foot in the house. It was Friday December 22nd and the Christmas holidays had begun. *My God, what a difference from a month ago when Kennedy bit the dust. The waters of the lake have closed over and X marks the spot.*

His dad would be working the afternoon shift Saturday and Sunday, but by some minor miracle he had scored the 25th and 26th as days of rest. Since he was a kid Billy couldn't remember his father being off on the Holiest of Hollies. Those big silver birds had to be in the air all three-hundred and sixty-five. Christmas dinner was often postponed, or brought forward, but the family didn't care as long a Mr. Carlsen was present to carve the golden brown turkey. His mother, a tear in her eye, would always say, "It's a blessing to have Harold at home anywhere near Christmas. During the war there were five without him."

Bill went up to his room and placed a well worn club bag beside the bed. He would go uptown to buy presents tomorrow. He tuned the radio to CFRB, 1010 on the dial, and heard the familiar jingle:

People's Credit Jewelers
Friendly Christmas shopping:

For the greater good of the listening audience, Wally Crouter reminded everyone that there was only one shopping day left. A message that caused most men to break out into a cold sweat.

When Bill came downstairs his mother was in the living room drinking a cup of tea. She was free as a bird till after boxing day, and was enjoying the luxury of putting her feet up.

"How did the exams go Billy?"

"Honestly Mom, I'm a little worried."

"You'll get through okay," she reassured.

"I guess we'll watch "Scrooge" Sunday night on TV, eh Mom?" He smiled broadly, wanting to leave school behind for the duration of the holidays.

"Why yes, what would Christmas be without a visit from Alastair Sim."

20

*

It was a glorious meal, shrimp cocktail for starters, turkey, mashed potatoes, a savory stuffing, gravy, peas, carrot and turnip, followed by plumb pudding with hard sauce for dessert. Bill's father treated himself to a glass of red wine while his mother and grandmother sipped on the leftover sherry that had been used to flavor the Christmas cake. When the table was finally cleared five bloated bellies managed to make it as far as the rec-room to watch "A Christmas Carol" on the families old faithful, black and white, seventeen inch, Westinghouse, console TV.

*

Early boxing day morning Bill gave Dave Graham a buzz on the landline. "Hey Tex, how'd you like to go skiing up in the Hockley Valley? My dad says I can have the Chevy for most of the day."

"Out of sight Billy. When can you pick me up?"

"I've got the skies in the car, so I could drop by your place in thirty minutes."

"Cool Slick. See ya later alligator."

"After a while crocodile."

Dave was waiting outside and wasted no time in putting his skies into the Biscayne. Both pairs were between the driver and passenger—tips suspended above the dash. Bill headed east to highway ten then booted it north to Orangeville. By ten o'clock he pulled into the parking lot of the Twin Hearths Ski club. They piled out of the car, paid for their lift tickets, strapped on the boards and headed for the rope tow.

Just as they were about to make their first run Dave pulled out a wine-skin and handed it to Bill. "Take a pull Carlsen, it'll put hair on your chest."

Billy squirted some of the amber liquid into his mouth and swallowed. He gasped audibly as tears began to form in the corners of his eyes. "What in hell kinda bingo is that?"

"A fine Seagrams VO," Dave answered, followed by wicked laugh. "It only burns for a little while."

"Okay Tex, try some of this," Bill rasped, while handing Dave a silver flask. Billy had sort of borrowed it from his grandmother, hoping she wouldn't look in the china cabinet before he got back.

"Holy Nellie Slick, what's in that stuff?" Dave began to cough, before handing the shinny hip hugger back to William Francis.

"Well, let's just say it contains grain spirits and cuts out the middle man." Some of the lab. alcohol was left over and he'd stuck a jam jar full of Sow U rocket fuel into his club bag before leaving the campus. Billy had mixed it fifty-fifty with water because the pure distillate would dissolve your throat.

*

By lunch time they could hardly stand up. The wine-skin and flask were both empty and for some reason it didn't seem to be cold at all. Trying to walk a straight line to reach the chalet's coffee shop counter was a challenge, but somehow Billy managed to order soup and sandwichs. They devoured the simple meal then fell asleep in front of the lodge's large fireplace. This was just as well when it came time for the drive back to Georgetown. Bill had the mother of all sore heads. Skiing can be very painful was the final thought that crossed his aching brain before falling asleep that night.

*

"Rise and shine, daylight in the swamp," his father harsh whispered, as he entered Billy's room early the next morning.

"Holy smokers Pop, it's still dark."

"I'd like to talk to you Sonny Jim before I go to work, so up and at 'em."

Bill slowly fought his way to the surface and managed to get both feet on the cold floor. His head felt like an over inflated medicine ball after the ski drunk, but he was able to stagger to the bathroom, wash his face, dress and make it down to the kitchen where his father was making bacon and eggs for breakfast. It was 6:00 am and Mr. Carlsen had to be on shift by eight.

Between mouthfuls of back bacon, toast and fried eggs Billy learned that his father had a lead on a '57 Chevy.

"Glenn Todd, at work, is buying a new car but the dealer won't give him diddley on a trade. He knows that you'd like to have a set of wheels and since we're friends he'll let it go for a hundred and fifty."

"No sale Pop, I've only got ninety-five in the bank and I couldn't afford the insurance."

"Okay Billy, here's the deal. Your mother and I will loan you the fifty-five difference. You can pay us back in the summer when you get a job." His father paused for a moment then smiled before adding, "Since we never got you a present for graduating from high school, we'll pick up the insurance till June."

His own car? That was for rich kids and the Carlsens were anything but. *What about gas and repairs? How would he manage?*

"That would be swell Dad but I really can't afford the operating expenses either."

"Granny has a little tucked away and she'll lend you what you need for gas and oil."

"That's a heck of nice thing for you all to do," Bill croaked, while shaking his father's hand.

*

It was a six cylinder, two tone, green and white Bel Air hardtop. It was the most beautiful thing that Billy had ever seen. His dad had phoned John Kirkwood the local insurance broker and paid for six months on the car. The Chevy was now legal to ply the roads of Ontario.

"She's a winner," Dave Graham whistled softy, two days later.

"I can hardly believe it Tex. This is a dream come true."

"Sure wish my old man would help me like that," Dave grumbled.

"Hey, you'll be able to find something in the summer."

"Yeah, but before that happens I've got to get through first year at Ryerson."

They piled into the Bel Air and headed across town to Perks Open Kitchen. The two boyhood pals plunked down into their favorite booth, then ordered fries with gravy and a cherry coke. It was snowing outside but it promised to be a light dusting.

*

Bill just about jumped out of his skin when he heard a familiar voice squeal, "Billy you're home."

"D-Doris it's been a long time," he stammered.

His high school sweetheart Doris Marshall was standing right beside him. When he got beyond the familiar pair of headlights packed into her tight sweater, Billy was aware of a navy blazered pipe sucker who had his right arm draped possessively around Doris.

"This is Lance Blublod," she gushed. "we just got pinned."

"Cheers there Lance," Dave muttered, while raising his fountain glass to eye level.

"Yeah, congratulations from me too," Billy chipped in, suddenly realizing he hadn't a lump in his throat. A sure sign of a checkout from Heartbreak Hotel.

"Nice running into you two." Doris waved like the Queen of England, before directing her prize catch towards a back booth.

When they'd finished their cokes and fries, Dave and Billy reckoned up at the cash register, then headed for the Chevy.

"I can't believe it Tex, no more magic spell."

"That's a good thing Slick. Doris sure is a looker, but she's got her sights fixed on the rich and famous."

"Right you are Davey me good man, and screw famous."

*

"Hey it's starting," Brenda shouted as Bill and his mother raced into the rec-room. They watched in awe while a sparkling crystal ball slowly descended down a vertical steel wire suspended high above Times Square. The telecast on WKBW Buffalo then cut to Guy Lombardo and his Royal Canadians playing "Auld Lang Syne", direct from the Waldorf Astoria. Nineteen sixty-four had been offically clocked in.

110

The next morning Bill hugged his mother, sister and grandmother, shook hands with his father, tossed the club bag into the back seat of the Bel Air and pointed the hood ornament in the general direction of Sowsbury. It had been a great holiday and boy, was this new set of wheels ever nifty.

21

William Francis knew he had to face the music sometime. Screwing up his last morsel of courage, he went over to Hogstroff to check the central bulletin board, attached to the long basement hallway wall, where first term marks were posted. Billy held his breath, as he approached the impartial lists, announcing victory or an early exit stage left. S.A.C. eh? Sacked At Christmas. Bill closed his eyes for a moment, crossed his fingers, then slowly raising a pair of trembling lids, focused on the short column of 'C's'.

"Holy cow," he gasped, "an average of 60.1 and no flunk bombs."

He was in. The great gods of academic pursuits had cast a benevolent thunderbolt from on high and William Francis was good to go for a second kick at the can.

*

"Hey, Carlsen that's one mean machine," Eddie hooted, while booting the front right.

"Yeah, I can hardly believe I have my own car."

"You know Billy, that wide back seat makes it a travelling motel."

"No chick's safe now. Maybe I should call it the lovemobile."

"Sheer genius Teddy, and I almost forgot to tell ya. I've christened my bug. From here on in it's not just a Volkswagen, how does Snoopy sound?"

"That's a good one Charlie Brown," Bill joked.

"So what are you going to name your Chevy?"

"I heard a spoofy tune on the way back about some Jewish cowboy. The title of the song was "Irving", and that's the handle I'm sticking on the '57.

"Sounds kinda weird to me Billy."

"Iriving," Bill crooned. "even on the range he carried two sets of dishes."

"You gotta be kidding?"

"Honest to God Eddie, that's part of the song."

A day later they were back at it. The only difference in their timetables was Inorganic Chemistry instead of Orgies and their first mandatory agricultural course, Animal Husbandry. The subject was taught by a legendary Prof. who'd been given the nickname Rust Hog. He was a short, slim, freckle faced, red head who tended to speak with a slow, broad, low pitched, Jimmy Stewart like drawl. An. Hub. classes were held in a tiny circular arena. Instead of an ice surface the concrete oblong floor was covered with sawdust. Tiers of hockey style folding seats rose from ringside to ten rows up. This was where the 4-H club of Sowsbury and the surrounding area showed their prize, cattle, sheep, goats and pigs during College Fair days in the fall and early spring.

Rust Hog had no use for city kids and referred to them as 'Yonge Street Farmers'. Anyone, who's home was on the range, was okay in his books and usually not given a hard time. Eddie and Bill arrived late for their first class and were centered out immediately by the loveable old carrot top.

"Well fellas, a little tardy are we? Your names please."

"S-Sorry sir, I'm Bill Carlsen

"It won't happen again Doctor McTavish, and my name's Ed Samson."

"Carlsen and Samson, kinda sounds like an old Vaudeville act. Now you two sit in the front row, and from now on try to figure out the mysteries of the big and little hands."

"Yes sir!" They replied in unison.
*

The lecture dealt with the various breeds of cattle that were common to Ontario farms. When Rust Hog got to Jerseys he paused for a moment then signaled for his assistant to bring a large cattle beast into the arena.

"This gentleman is a prize Jersey bull, and I-I think the honour of showing him today should go to Mr. Carlsen."

Billy got up and reluctantly made his way to the middle of the ring. The grinning assistant passed the lead rope to an apprehensive William Francis and slowly walked away.

"Now Mr. Samson, you'll be the clean up man, while your partner guides this fine specimen around the ring."

Eddie didn't have a clue as to what Rust Hog was talking about, until he was handed a flat bladed shovel and directed to the rear end of the bull. Billy started to pull on the rope to get the huge animal underway but the stubborn creature just stood there, all four feet firmly planted. The rest of the class started to laugh and whistle. The big Jersey, seeming to appreciate the cheers from his audience, looked up toward the stands, then let out a king-sized fart, preparatory to depositing two sloppy plops on the sawdust floor.

"Get to work Samson and shovel it!" McTavish ordered.

Eddie did as he was told, then stood there dumbfounded with the steaming mass of cow pies resting on the metal blade. "Where do I put it sir?"

Rust Hog pointed to a large garbage can resting against the side boards. Eddie placed his prize in the container and returned to the ready position. Billy figured there was only one way to get the bulls attention, so he turned around quickly and pinched the beast's nose. The bewildered critter looked at Bill with his large, expressionless brown eyes and slowly began to move. Ed followed at a respectful distance while Billy led the Jersey twice around the ring.

*

"Not too bad for a Yonge Street farmer," Rust Hog admitted, when Billy got back to the starting line.

"May we sit down now sir?" Eddie all but pleaded.

"W-We get the point sir," William Francis quavered.

"Okay fellas, but from now on be on time and don't ditch any of my lectures."

*

They both nodded, then made a beeline for their seats. The assistant continued the show by bringing in a Holstein milker, followed by a Hereford steer and several other breeds. After explaining the difference between a bull and a steer Rust Hog stated loudly, "Now gentleman, aren't you glad that most of you are still bulls."

While unconsciously crossing their legs, the scarlet faced Aggies dutifully snickered. Ten minutes later a collective sigh of relief sounded when Dr. McTavish stated that it was time for them to get on to their next class.

Bill, still shaken up from his first encounter with a large animal, walked slowly towards the Physics building.

"Well one thing for sure Eddie, I'd never make a farmer.

"Yeah, at home we grow cash crops. Shoveling cow crap is new for me too," Edward H. groused, experiencing an instant replay of his short course in bovine scatology.

*

At lunchtime they found out that chipped beef on toast was the Barfman noontime offering. One look at this delectable dish caused Eddie, now a little green around the gills, to jump up and head for the red Exit sign.

22

The city of Sowsbury had plunged through the gates of hell, and was without a shadow, the home of the devil incarnate—according to several local church groups. The evil citizenry had answered 'Yes' to a question put forth in the November municipal elections. Sowsbury, the good, would now be allowed to have cocktail lounges. The first to take advantage of this sinful situation were the wicked owners of the Empire Hotel. Their large basement had been renovated by a clever carpenter and the brand, spanking new 'Furnace Room' was open for business on January the fifteenth.

*

One big advantage of this den of earthly delights was; men could go there without a lady in tow, sit in the same room as the female of the species, and if the stars had aligned themselves correctly, meet up with a fair damsel who might desire a modicum of masculine company. Definitely a quantum leap in the assent of man. The Vets, Aggies and Udderson girls were the first to take advantage of this wanton display of loose morality. Sex makes the world go round, sells soap, cars and B movies at the Odeon.

*

Thursday night, the dynamic duo of Samson and Carlsen entered the dark, dank caverns of Hades. The pipes running from the hotel's steam boiler were left exposed below the ceiling and the walls had been given a cave-like appearance by applying swirls of rough plaster. A true artistic genius had painted everything red and black. Old Beelzebub would have been right at home if he'd decided to make a guest appearance.

"Over here Billy," Donna and Alice, called out when they spotted Ed and Bill.

"Hi Alice!" Eddie smiled. "Boy, is it ever good to see you again."

"How was your holiday?" she bubbled, thinking that Edward H. Samson was indeed a handsome fellow.

"You know, it was kinda of strange. I enjoyed Christmas and all, but after boxing day I was counting the hours till I got back to good old Hay Seed U."

"Me too!" Billy chimed in.

"How about we order a round of boiler makers," Donna suggested after the two boys sat down.

"Okay ladies, you've got me on that one," Billy confessed.

"A bottle of beer, a shot of whiskey and a large glass," Alice explained.

They caught a waiters attention and placed their order. Several minutes later he returned with the drinks. Billy tipped the tray totter two bits, hoping to avoid any problems with ID. He had Pete's birth certificate, but a little coin of the realm usually greased the fire pole.

"Now here's how you do it," Alice demonstrated by half-filling her glass with suds, then dropping in the shot glass containing the rye.

"Holy smoke, is that ever neat," Eddie whooped, while plunking his shot glass into a pool of foamy brew.

The combination of beer and whiskey proved to be a potent mixture. After the third round of 'makers' the giggling guzzlers were jet streaming higher than a 707 at cruising altitude.

Ed, who'd started to grow a goatee and mustache, excused himself before heading to the can. He was halfway there when one of the waiters stood in his path and began to laugh.

"Okay I'll bite," Eddie prompted. "What's so funny?"

Looking at the emerging hairs on Ed's upper lip and chin, the barrel chested suds slinger snickered, "I've got one of those at home but it doesn't have teeth in it."

"I guess your boyfriend must have had them all out at the dentists then," Eddie shot back.

"Hey college boy, are you calling me a fag or somethin'."

"Nope, simply having a little fun, just like you."

Eddie, a solidly built six footer, remained calm and self assured.

He hadn't told anyone, including Billy, that his sport at home was karate and he held a black belt.

"Okay then corn brain, let's go into the gents and continue our little conversation."

"Look mister I don't want any hassles, so why don't we call it a draw and enjoy the rest of the night."

"Chicken are you college boy?" the burly waiter sneered.

"Gosh no, I'm just an Aggie from the S.A.C.," Eddie countered, before stepping around the waiter and entering the washroom. The surly server was right behind him.

*

They were now alone in the two stall facility and very close to one another. Eddie waiting for the beefy bartender to make the first move, had a brain flash.

"Just before we start I want to show you something, if that's all right with you."

"Sure kid, but after that I'm going to tear you apart."

At rocket speed, Eddie turned sideways and delivered a roundhouse kick that tore a stall door off its hinges. He then swung around to the attack position. Using his lightning quick right hand Ed grabbed the shirt collar of the startled waiter.

"I was all Ontario last year in my class and next year I'll have to register my hands as deadly weapons. If it's okay with you, we could just shake on it and go our separate ways. Whattaya say chief?"

"Y-Yeah," his stocky opponent gasped, while Eddie tightened his grip.

"Put her there partner," Eddie said confidently, before shaking the man's hand.

"No hard feelings then?" the frightened waiter squeaked as he edged towards the door.

"None at all," Eddie affirmed, stepping purposefully towards one of the urinals.

When he returned to the table Billy asked him why he'd taken so long.

"Just a little chat about hockey with one of the employees of this four star establishment, William my good man."

"You're a riot Eddie," Alice snorted.

"I'll bet there's more to it than that," Billy mused openly.

*

The Furnace Room was allowed, under the new regulations, to have entertainment. A small stage had been erected at the far end of the lounge and at nine o'clock the show began with a homegrown country and western group: 'Hank Slush and His Flying Brakemen'. They did hurtin' and honky-tonk songs that would've brought tears to the eyes of a serial killer. This, along with the smoky, blue layer hanging below the ceiling was enough to make a Kleenex salesman a firm believer in the power of, "Your Cheatin' Heart".

Bill and Ed had meant to go home early and get some scabbing in before the study lamp went dim, but like most best laid plans, it was the last call that brought things to a crashing halt. When the lights were flashed twice the two couples got up and made their way to the parking lot.

"I'd really like to drive you back to campus in my new Chevy, Donna."

"Okay Teddy, you're on," Donna purred seductively.

"See you two lovebirds later," Alice coverd a yawn, as she and Eddie headed for her T-Bird.

In a cloud of dust and a hearty Hi ho Irving, the General's pride of '57 and one of your Fix Or Repair Daily's departed in different directions.

*

William Francis had found a safe place to park behind the beef barns. He'd been told by Gary Barker that Trigger never checked there, since the entrance was gated and locked. This obviously meant that no one could get into the area. There was, however, one small item that had been overlooked. Gary's best friend Joey Armstrong, who did odd jobs for Rust Hog, required a key to the kingdom in order check on the cattle and Bill had been loaned the 'Open Sesame' for the night.

"Boy does that perfume ever smell good," Billy whispered, shortly after shuting off the engine.

"It's called Boucheron," Donna murmured.

"You know, over the holidays every time I had a free moment, I kept thinking of you."

"That's strange Billy, because you were on my mind a lot too."

"You're so beautiful Donna," he gasped.

"Billy I want you right here right now, it's been so long," she moaned deep in her throat.

In the wee hours of Friday morning, with the outside temperature hovering just above the freezing mark, Irving's spacious back seat proved to be a valuable asset. Billy was still in that stage of his life where his brain ran a direct circuit to a rather sensitive external organ. It's always amazing to look into the future, but like most men, this chronic condition would plague William Francis well into his middle years.

Perhaps Kitty, Billy's former flame, had summed things up perfectly when they were driving up to her parents cottage in the Muskokas.

"You know Teddy, men are really very simple. They're usually horny, hungry or sleepy, so my philosophy is; if he doesn't have an erection and has just gotten up from a nap, then feed him a bacon sandwich."

For some strange reason, at the time, Billy was neither hungry or sleepy.

120

23

Come the harsh reality of a dark, snowy, winters morning, it was with deep regret, lack of snooze time, and one too many wobbley pops, that Terrible Teddy arrived twenty minutes late for another eight o'clock. Fortunately the Basic Botany lecture hall was the size of the O'Kefee Centre, and he managed to tiptoe to a seat right next to Pete, while Professor Rosebud, king of the plant world, peered myopically downwards trying to change an acetate on the overhead projector.

*

"Well bless my soul, if ain't sleeping beauty," Pete whispered, as a hungover, camel mouthed, aching Aggie Carlsen, collapsed onto a hard, plastic chair.

"Don't start roomie, I'm not in the mood to be mothered."

"A little testy are we Billy?"

"Sorry Pete. I know it must be a bummer for you. Some asshole who stumbles in well past midnight wouldn't be a starter on my team either."

"Okay, then listen up, and tune in to the developing mysteries of photosynthesis."

William Francis was asleep at the switch when the lecture ended and would have gladly stayed in the lights out mode but for a poke in the ribs from good Aggie Eastman. The morning droned on and by lunchtime Billy was riding on the fumes. A greasy grilled cheese, garnished with a wilted dill pickle, was all he could manage at Barthman.

*

The afternoon extravaganza included a qualitative chemistry lab. where rotten egg gas was used to remove metals from a clear colorless liquid. At the first whiff of over the hill, prenatal chicken, William Francis was finished, and spent a great deal of time blazing a trail from the work benches to the washroom in the basement of the Chemistry building. The experiment was a long one and by the time they'd finished it was time for supper.

Billy, however, had no appetite, and went straight back to 301 to catch up on some much needed shut-eye. He'd barely gotten past lay me down to sleep when all aspirations of forty winks came to a juddering halt.

"Hey, Carlsen get up, there's something big going on over at Udderson," Eddie hollered, while urgently shaking Rip Van William by the shoulder.

"Leave me alone Samson, I'm fatally fatigued."

"Rumor has it, the An. Hub. boys have let a bull loose in Virgin City."

"A cattle beast in the girls residence?"

"That's the scoop, Teddy me boy."

"Holy jumpin', I've got to see this." Billy bolted upright, and rushed for the door.

"Hey wait for me," Eddie shouted, astonished by the speeding bullet that was already halfway to the staircase.

The gigantic Hereford had rampaged in the foyer of Our Lady of Perfect Pastries for nearly an hour by the time Bill and Ed joined the crowd of well wishers gathered at the yawning portals of the Box Office—as the less than sensitive Aggies called it. Women's Lib. had yet to make it's mark at Sowsbury. Barefoot and pregnant was still a catch phrase amongst the good old boys of the S.A.C. As far as they were concerned, men were men and the babes trained to make pies and cookies were thankful for it.

Furniture had been overturned, curtains torn to confetti, and a pile of cow plops as big as the Royal York had been deposited on the tile floor. Everyone present was having a great time except the house mothers, who'd achieved a state of screaming hysteria, and were perched precariously on top of the large reception desk. A rat running loose in the building would likely have created the same concern. The fair protectors of the kingdom all hailed from the city.

The lovely ladies of Home Ec., gathered on the big set of stairs that led to the second floor, were continually cheering on old Ferdinand who'd occasionally bellow appreciatively in their direction.

Dr. Udderson, herself, finally appeared on the scene. She was a determined woman and knew exactly what to do. The cool, queen of the kitchen and tasty tarts, grabbed the nearest phone to call the only one she knew who could save the day. No, it wasn't Mighty Mouse, as some might have predicted. She'd gone person to person with Rust Hog.

*

"Stand aside you bunch of Yonge Street farmers," the blotch faced, carrot top thundered as he elbowed his way up the steps to the heavy oak doors of Our Lady.

The shinning knight of the Animal Husbandry Department had arrived wearing faded green overalls, a pair of gumboots and carrying a one gallon galvanized bucket.

"Over here Herbert," Flora Udderson cried, when she spied her rescuer.

"Don't worry, I'll have that no good son-of-a-bull out of here in three shakes."

Dr. Herbert Mctavish, holding the metal pail firmly in the curled fingers of his outstretched right arm, carefully approached the pawing mammoth. The snorting animal sniffed the air cautiously, then appeared to set himself for a charge.

"Suck, suck, hey boss, hey boss," Rust Hog called softly.

"Herbert, what in the devil are you doing?" Flora roared.

"This is an old trick my father taught me. Now go stand behind that desk and watch what happens."

The head home wrecker did as she was told, the crow's feet around her eyes widening to match a look of incredulous amazement when the bull suddenly became docile and followed Rusty out of the building. The King of Cattle, now playing the role of the pied piper of Sowsbury, led the big Hereford all the way back to the beef barns. The astonished crowd of spectators tagged along and could hardly believe what they'd just witnessed.

The stock of Doc Herbert McTavish had suddenly soared to top spot on the Aggie Index. It was another moment that would live till the end of days in Cow U. folklore.

Maybe not as satisfying as beer in the milk coolers, but for those who were present they could always say: "Mind the time that old Rust Hog tamed the beast."

*

The fallout, from the bull in the china shop incident, was directed at the graduating year. They, as a group, had fessed up to the stunt and took full responsibility. No one knew for sure who brought the Hereford up from the cattle pens and let him loose in the foyer, but every time Charlie Ross told the story it was hard for him to keep the I and me out of it. Once again the long arm of the law reached into the pockets of the senior classmen. Fifteen bucks a head seemed rather steep, but it did pay for the clean up of Udderson, with a little left over to bolster the Dean's scholarship fund.

When questioned about how he'd managed to get the colossal bovine out of the foyer the Rusted One explained in his best Jimmy Stewart drawl.

" W-Well fellas, it's this way. I put salt and a little maple syrup in the pail. The old bull liked the smell of it and wanted some. He put his head down and followed me back to the O.K. coral. Just a little country know how that would be beyond your average 'Yonge Street' farmer."

Dr. Herbert B. McTavish, had become a walking, talking legend, and would be an inspiration for Aggies yet to be born.

124

24

*

Bullroar, bull session, bull market, bullish, and bull crap were the catch words for days to come at the Cow College. Each utterance would cause eyes to roll, funny bones to be tickled, and of course, blasts of uproarious laughter. The incident quickly faded into the deep, distant past, and two weeks later the hottest topic on campus centered around the annual shindig at St. Alfred's. It was odd that the local hospital would cause such excitement amongst the Aggies and Vets, but after all, it did have a highly acclaimed school of nursing.

*

That's right, three-hundred females dedicated to the healing arts. Serious, studious young ladies who knew how to take care of the human body. The boys of the S.A.C. and V.D.C. all figured they qualified, given most were indeed, in need, of tender loving care. The F.U.C. girls hoped that cookies and butter tarts would carry the day. As one of Udderson's finest put it, "If you want to be treated properly then go see a doctor, not some slut of a husband hunting Florence Nightingale."

*

"Hey Billy, are you going tonight?"

"Wild horses Eddie."

"Yeah, me too, some of the stories I hear from the seniors are right out of *Playboy*."

"You mean the babes at St. Al's are that hot."

"Well let's put it this way Carlsen, all they've seen for the last several months are their classmates and the nursing sisters. They're ripe for the plucking."

"Or something in rhyme," Billy hee-hawed, before turning towards Pete. "Are you coming?"

"No way José, Tova would never speak to me again if I did. Maybe you should consider Donna on this one as well."

"Relax Pete, as my Uncle Ole would say,"It don't matter where ya work up yer appetite as long as ya eat at home."

"What's a matter Eastman? Ya wanna be a virgin all your life?" Ed prodded.

"Don't worry Samson, just consider me one of those guys who prefers to dine *à la maison*," Pete stated innocently.

"So Steady Eddie," Billy chuckled. "Your wheels or mine?"

"You play chauffeur Carlsen, Irving has the most room."

*

The large recreation hall in the basement of St. Alfreds had been decorated with hundreds of helium balloons and a barge load of colored crape paper. The lights were turned down low and a first class Hi-Fi system, complete with a DJ, was providing the music. Paul McCutcheon, who worked for the local radio station CSOW, behind the microphone. Tables and chairs had been set up at right angles to the red brick walls, and a large dance floor lay in between. It was open season on Nurses, Vets and Aggies.

*

No alcohol was permitted at the dance, but two large punch bowls had been stationed at the end of the hall with an overflowing plate of cookies right beside them. Bill and Eddie knew what to expect from the dry as a dust bunny hospital residence, so they decided to improvise.

The inside pocket of a sports coat has many uses, one of which is hiding a mickey of lab. alcohol. The magic moonshine had worked in Wonderland and with any luck it would be party pleaser in Nurseville. While no one was looking Eddie, followed by Billy, emptied the contents of their twelve ounce bottles into the lovely cut crystal vessels containing the lemonade and orange juice.

*

For a while, nothing seemed to be happening as the nurses and supervising nuns tippled the delicious beverages from the glass bowls. Sister Joan, who was normally very reserved, began to tap her feet to the Beatles hit song "Love me do." She suddenly grabbed Sister Marry-Kate's hand and hauled her on to the dance floor. They were a little to slow to start but once they got going, it was full speed ahead.

The rollicking pair of jiving penguins astonished the crowd and could have carried off first prize on American Bandstand. When the song finished the appreciative audience gave them a resounding ovation, and from there on in, the boy meets girl sock hop was a huge success.

William Francis was content to watch the fun until he spotted a dark haired beauty sitting at a table by the door. Her hair was short, and done in a very fashionable Sassoon blunt cut. She was wearing a strapless black dress and matching stiletto pumps. Bill gathered up his nerve and went over to ask her to dance.

"Billy Carlsen at your service Miss," he quipped.

"That's quite an opener Billy."

"I'll bet you a million bucks you're a nurse," he continued.

"Okay, now I'm rich. Pay up college boy."

"I thought everyone in the hall was an RN or a gonna-be."

"Wrong again, I'm taking a course here in the Bacteriology Department."

"Well live and learn. W-Would you care to dance?" Bill stammered, suddenly feeling unsure of himself.

"With pleasure Prince Charming," she cooed happily.

The positive response of the bodacious Bacteriologist helped Billy to regain his confidence, as he guided her smoothly across the floor to the strains of an old Percy Faith instrumental. "Theme From a Summer Place" had always been one of his favorites and by the end of the record they were up close and personal. Billy was about to ask her for another dance when Charlie Ross cut in. Bill liked Charlie and politely stepped aside. William Francis had returned to his seat near the DJ's table before realizing that he hadn't asked her name.

The spiked punch seemed to have loosened things up, and by the last dance many of the Aggies and Vets, who'd arrived alone, were now heading to the exit sign with female company. Billy tried to find the raven haired Cinderella that he'd met earlier, but she'd already disappeared. Lucky Charlie he thought to himself.

Eddie hadn't connected with anyone either. Feeling like a couple of rejects, who didn't make the team, they left the hospital and drove back to Hereford in Irving.

"I met this real babe and you know, I forgot to get her name?"

"Jeez Carlsen, you've been working too hard."

"I think they enjoyed the punch though Eddie."

"Yeah, we managed to liven things up, but a fat lot of good that did us."

"Well at least the nunny bunnies and pan porters had a good time."

"You know Billy, I wouldn't be surprised if sainthood's your true destiny."

"And screw you too, oh king of the suitcase."

"What in hell's that supposed to mean, Teddy two shoes."

"Samsonite you knucklehead."

"Sorry I asked."

*

Irving made it back to campus carrying his load of frustrated Aggies. It wasn't easy being a car in the early sixties, especially when you were manufactured in nineteen-fifty-seven. What, with all that salt they put on the roads during Ontario winters, it was a miracle to last ten years before the dreaded wrecker came and towed you to the junk yard. Most dogs in the province had it better eh?

128

25

Bill couldn't get her out of his mind and decided to take the direct approach. Saturday morning, after breakfast, he fired up Irving and drove over to St. Alfred's. The nursing sister at the information desk told him that he, couldn't under any circumstance short of a doctor's order for a test, enter the hallowed waiting room of the hospital's laboratory. Bill figured this was just an administrative bluff and eventually found his way to the section of the second floor, clearly marked on the directory in the foyer as the Department of Medical Technology. The waiting room was located across from the elevator.

*

Billy boldly approached the receptionist, a plan already formed in his mind. "Excuse me Miss have you seen my sister?"

"And who might that be?" The lady behind the desk asked in a friendly manner.

"Brenda Carlsen ma'am, I'm suposed to meet Sis here, then drive her home after she has her tests."

"She hasn't arrived yet, but you can have a seat over there young man."

Bill hoped he might spot his mystery lady, if she passed across this sacred ground, on her way to a class or the wards. He'd been to the Georgetown hospital once for a TB x-ray, but that was all he knew about this end of the medical profession. Billy sat for an hour but didn't see the black haired goddess from the night before. *Maybe if I had one of her shoes, I could pull the same trick as the Prince did in that Walt Disney movie I saw when I was a kid.*

He was reaching and he knew it. Ten additional minutes limped by before William Francis decided to leave. Head down, Bill passed the hospital cafeteria, and realized he was starving—his nose drawn like a magnet to a steel culvert by the olfactory teasers wafting from the kitchen. Billy got in line and ordered Shepherd's Pie, the special of the day.

He sat at a table alone and was about to leave when *she* walked through the door, then proceeded to a large coffee urn next to the cash. Bill waited for her to sit down, before he went over to say hello.

"You know that stuff has caffeine in it?"

"Well that sure is different from Billy Carlsen at your service," she replied, widdening her bright hazel eyes.

Bill grinned sheepishly. "Gee whiz you remembered. I kinda goofed last night and forgot to ask your name."

"Ellen Howard." The Ava Gardner look-a-like smiled.

"Is Charlie Ross your boyfriend?" he asked, wanting to clear the air.

"No, we're just old friends from back home. If you'd done your homework you could have found out that Sandi Coulter in Udderson '65 is wearing his class ring."

"In that case Ellen, how'd you like to go for a drive tomorrow afternoon."

"Sorry Billy duty calls, but I'm off next Saturday."

"Okay then, let's take in the hockey game at Guernsey Gardens. Guelph will be in town to play the Woodchucks."

"I'll look forward to that, but you'll have to excuse me, I've a practical to prepare for, like ten minutes ago."

"Okay,I'll pick you up at noon, or is that too early?"

"That'll be fine," Ellen shouted over her shoulder, exiting the cafeteria faster than the dust cloud of the roadrunner escaping from the drooling coyote—or if you perfer, Little Red Riding Hood making her getaway from the big bad wolf.

*

Sunday night Bill, with Pete in tow, decided to go down to Hereford's common room and catch a little eye before assuming the horizontal. It was Sunday February 9, 1964. A day that would live forever in the minds of a multitude of mortals, who inhabited planet earth at that juncture in time and space. As they entered the darkened room, where the TV was located, Ed Sullivan was saying...."the city has never witnessed the excitement stirred up by these youngsters from Liverpool who call themselves the Beatles."

The image of a hundred hysterical maidens, producing sounds that would make a thousand howling police cars seem like a quite day in the park, flashed on the screen a moment before the camera picked up the four mop-haired Brits who stared to wail about someone loving them ya, ya, ya. Every time the camera focused on Ringo—his facial expressions resembling those of a frightened puppy on its way to the pound—the Aggies gathered in the common room guffawed and snorted like a barnyard full of Yorkshire pigs.

"So what's all the excitement about?" Billy whispered. "They look like a bunch of freaks to me."

"Carlsen, these guys are the hottest thing there is. I've got three of their forty-fives."

"Yeah Pete, and you can keep 'em. Give me good old folk music anytime."

"The Kingston who?" Pete snickered, as he moved closer to the big, twenty-one inch Admiral that projected a brilliant picture in full SpectraVision.

Bill was amazed when he was told that four out of the five songs performed by the Beatles had been written by John Lennon and Paul McCartny. Billy played a little guitar himself and had to admit that George Harrison was pretty fair with the axe. By the end of the "really big shew" William Francis was starting to come around to Pete's estimation. "These guys were darned good, and might be around for awhile."

The 'fab four' finished up with "I Want to Hold Your Hand" and were given a screaming send off by the horde of frenzied females who'd been lucky enough to get tickets to witness the beginning of the British invasion. Before signing off Ed announced that the Beatles would be featured on his show for the following two Sundays. An open invitation to the eighty-one million people in the United States and Canada watching that night, to rotate their TV antennas towards the nearest CBS station in the up coming weeks.

*

"They're so friggin' great," Pete exploded, when they returned to 301.

"Hey Pete, you just said friggin'."

"Oh shit, I-I mean shoot, if Tova heard me talking like this it'd be curtains."

"Welcome to the real world Eastman," Billy grunted, before turning out the light.

*

The same old, same old, seemed to be the case for the next six days. All Billy's classes were going fine except for non-orgies. The course required a modicum of mathematical skills and this was not a gift that had been bestowed upon our young hero. Funnily enough, he was doing well in An. Hub. After a rocky start, William Francis had developed a keen interest in horses, sheep, and cattle. He was actually starting to enjoy Rust Hog's classes, and laughed along with everyone else when the celebrated matador proclaimed one morning, with modicum of double entendre, "You know boys, the price of pork is sky high these days and a lot a farmers are getting into pigs." The old, freckle faced bull buster from Cowplop Township had become the resident wit of Sow U.

*

The OA/OV Redmen from Guelph, Sowsbury's arch-rivals, seemed to be able to score at will and if it wasn't for Gary Barker's hat trick the final tally would have been seven zip. Ellen and Billy had a great time at the game and lasted until the halfway mark of the third period when they left Guernsey Gardens to have a drink at the Furnace Room. They found a table near the bar and ordered two rye and gingers.

"How old are you Billy?" she asked after William Francis showed Pete's ID to the waiter.

"Turned the big two-one last summer," he bluffed like a gambler holding a losing hand.

"Strange thing, the name I noticed on the birth certificate you just flashed was Pete something or other."

"Okay, here's the straight goods. My name's actually Peter William Carlsen, but I didn't like the first one. It kinda reminds you of a saint or something and that's why I chose to go by the middle one."

Ellen wrinkled her brow for a moment before saying, "I hope you never become a used car salesman. You'd starve to death!"

"All right then, you've got me. That was my roomie's plastic passport and I just turned sixteen. I'm what you might call a child prodigy."

She started to laugh. "Maybe I was wrong. You wouldn't happen to have a '50 Meteor on your lot? The one your grandmother only drove to church on Sundays."

"Shot down in flames again, I'm twenty and still learning to shave."

"That's okay Billy, because I really like your sense of humor. I started training when I was seventeen, and I just turned twenty myself last week."

"Holy cow, that makes me older than you. Hey, maybe we could go to the movies some evening soon."

"That's another problem, my course is finished and I've have to be back in Ottawa next Friday."

His face dropped like a runaway elevator. "You've gotta be kidding! I-I thought you'd be here till the spring."

"Nope, but I'll give you my phone number, and if you're ever in the nation's capital then give me a call."

"Well, you never know your luck Miss Howard," he replied stoically, as she handed him a neatly folded piece of paper.

*

Billy said good-bye to Ellen on the steps of the hospital's residence, then drove at a leisurely pace back to the campus. She was some piece of work, however, Bill figured his chances of seeing her again were slim to none. Ottawa wasn't exactly the back of the moon, but he knew that a job at home would likely keep him pinned down for most of the summer. "Boy she sure is beautiful," he sighed plaintively.

Billy didn't understand why, but he had a strange premonition that Ellen Howard was to be an important part of his life. "Yeah, and someday there'll be an NHL team in Florida," he muttered to himself, realizing that El Predicto had never won a batting title.

26

The slate grey sky and light snowfall had kept Billy confined in his room the following Saturday morning. Pete was visiting an uncle who lived in Sarnia and Billy was all by his lonesome in 301. It wasn't all that bad because it gave William Francis a chance to bone up on some of the hidden meanings in *Pilgrim's Progress*. They sure as hell were buried deep in this boring chunk of literary refuse—mind you that was only Billy's opinion. In fact, their English Prof. had all but swooned when he discussed the allegorical gems contained between the covers of Bunyan's 17th century masterpiece. Different strokes for different folks was one way of looking at it Bill thought, or maybe it was simply bullshit baffles brains.

*

Billy the Kid and Paul Bunyan, then again, maybe it was John, but who really gave a flying fig, called it quits when Ed poked his head through the open door of the Carlsen-Eastman royal suite.

"Making any progress?" Eddie deadpanned.

"Hey, that's pretty clever for a guy who's only made two English lectures this term," Billy chuckled.

"Yeah, but I have the *Monarch Outlines* on the good Pilgrim, so why go to class."

Billy was well aware of Steady Eddie's eidetic memory and knew that he could likely quote most of the stuff he'd read verbatim. "Okay genius boy, then what we should do is check out of this flea bag and get some fresh air."

"Now you're talking Carlsen, but I've got a better idea. Let's hop in the Bug and drive over to Mary Hill. It's just a whistle stop but they've got two pubs there."

"Say the secret word and win a hundred dollars." Billy fluttered his eyebrows—Groucho take note eh?

Eddie immediately looked up at the ceiling to see if a duck was about to descend with a C-note clamped in its beak. Since nothing drifted down from the rafters, Edward H. motioned towards the yawning portal of 301.

Forty-five minutes later the sun had broken through the overcast, but a raw north wind was still pushing scurrying wisps of powdery snow across the blacktop. Hands cupped over their ears and teeth chattering they climbed out of Eddie's Beetle. As advertised, there were two hotels in the village of Mary Hill, one on one side of the main drag, and the other directly across. Each of the gilded watering holes boasted a men's beverage room and an L&E. The hell bent for eats and drinks Freshmen chose the larger of the two hostelries because of its restaurant. The big hand and little hand were well past the vertical and "Chowtime" had rocketed to number one on the CHUM top forty.

"Okay boys, show us your ID," a brassy, gum chewing waitress demanded before she would serve them.

"Here's mine!" Bill smiled winningly, while handing over Pete's birth certificate.

"And this is my proof," Eddie piped up, proudly presenting the fake document he'd won in a poker game during his high school days.

The frizzy haired, bleached-blonde, fat-rolled burger slinger hesitated for a moment before saying, "I guess youse guys is all right, but if the cops come in, I'd suggest a quick trip to the gents."

"Thank you ma'am," Billy responded respectfully, remembering that Frank Sinatra had said, to always treat a dame like a lady and a lady like a dame or something like that. Besides, he liked Kim Novak a lot better than Frank when he'd seen "Pal Joey" at the Odeon.

The menu contained several interesting items including the daily special, button ribs, sauerkraut and fried potatoes. This sounded like a winner to Ed and Bill and they both ordered *le plat du jour*—not too shabby for someone with six years of high school French eh? They washed down the full fat overload with several glasses of lager and at the end of the feast, the chock-full Aggies promptly loosened their belts.

"Boy was that ever good," Billy groaned contentedly, as he carefully wiped grease from his lips.

135

"I don't think I'll be able to eat for a week," Ed sighed, before lighting up a Craven A.

"That sauerkraut with the fresh pepper was a real fireball," Billy projected a rolling thunder belch.

"Yeah, and the mountain of spuds that went with it was out of sight."

"It was the bacon bits they added Eddie, that made it taste so good."

"Well, one thing for sure Billy, we'll never get grub like this at Barfman."

*

Having tried out the delights of one hotel, Eddie and Billy decided to wander over to the second joint that was much smaller than the place where they'd had lunch. The Men's side resembled a large farmhouse dinning room with several tables placed along three of the four walls. The fourth had an opening into the kitchen. When Ed and Bill looked at a laminated menu card, that was propped up against a Heinz ketchup bottle, it was plain to see that hamburgs, hot dogs and hot sandwiches were the featured items of this four star establishment. The waiter didn't hassle them about ID and before you could say Jackie Robinson four glasses of ale appeared, like rabbits from a silk top hat, in the middle of the circular, yellow, arborite table where they were seated.

"Take one for yourself," Billy said, while motioning towards the pile of change in front of them.

"Thanks kid!" the waiter grinned openly. "Relax fella's the O.P.P never check here."

The two Frosh exhaled a lungful of relief and began to savour the ice cold beer that the jovial suds merchant had left on the table. Knowing that the Ontario Provincial Police wouldn't be patrolling the town in their overgrown bubble gum machines was good news to the under aged Aggies.

Billy looked up as the door to the beverage room opened and was astonished to see two, full bearded Mennonite farmers, dressed in wide brimmed, black hats and turn of the century well worn, black suits, enter the pub.

136

They were carrying wicker baskets and stopped at a corner table nearest the kitchen. The three men sitting there, being locals, knew that the farmers were selling fresh eggs. Each of the trio laid out a dime and grabbed several eggs from the basket held by the younger of the two Anabaptist sod busters. Seconds later three eggs had been cracked on the rim of their beer glasses and plopped into the foamy lager. Without blinking an eye the stodgy brew was chug-a-luged—canary yokes, whites and all.

"Wouldja getta load of that?" Billy whispered.

"That's a new one on me," Eddie murmured.

"Hey Samson, whattaya say we give it a try?"

"You're on Billy!"

When the black-clad farmers came over to the Aggies table, Bill and Ed dug deep into their blue jeans then plunked two well worn dimes onto the arborite surface. The Mennonites thanked them, and since there were no further requests for eggs they left the hotel.

Eddie banged his egg on the side of the table before hoisting it over the beer glass. He then split the shell and the slimy contents oozed drippingly into the carbonated brew. Billy followed suit and seconds later they attempted to down the slippery concoction. Billy's egg stuck like a lump of lead in his throat and he reflexively up-chucked the gooey mess back into his glass. Ed swallowed the entire contents of his glass and pushed back, his lips curving upwards in an impish smile. Billy, however, sat there red faced and couldn't bring himself to try for another attempt at a down-the-hatcher.

"Got caught in your throat eh Billy?" Eddie gloated.

"Yeah, I was doing okay until my Adam's apple got in the way," William Francis gasped, a little watery eyed.

"No sweat Carlsen. Hey, listen to those guys over there."

Eddie had pointed to the table by the kitchen where the three men sat, who'd also bought eggs from the Mennonite farmers. One of them was broadcasting in a loud voice, "I'll betcha that no one in this room can eat a raw egg, shell and all, especially someone who just ralphed up his cookies."

Billy knew they were talking about him and he was ticked off. Without thinking he yelled at the big mouth who'd made the bet, "I'll take you up on that one mister."

"Okay sonny, but lets make it interesting. If you can't put the egg in your mouth and chew it up without opening your trap then you owe me a saw buck."

Young master Carlsen had been painted into corner and he knew it. Mustering up all the bravado he could Billy squeaked, "No problem sir, let's get started."

The man rose from his chair and Eddie was startled to see that he was a six foot plus, two-hundred and fifty pounder. Towering over Bill the big farmer snarled, "Hand over the ten spot kid and we'll let the bartender hold the money."

Bill dug into his wallet but could only find five dollars. He looked at Ed for help and was relieved when Eddie pulled out a matching picture of the Queen. The ham fisted giant grabbed the cash and handed it to the waiter who smiled knowingly. *Oh, oh, Bill thought, they've done this before.*

"All right then kid, here's the egg."

*

Bill knew that he had to act fast and not think about what he was going to do. He opened his mouth wide and jammed the egg between his teeth, then with lips firmly sealed, Bill bit down hard and began to chew. It was all he could do to keep his mouth shut and to stop himself from choking. Billy gathered up every ounce of determination he could and munched madly on the revolting mess in his mouth. With a supreme effort William Francis swallowed the shell bits, yoke and white. His eyes glazed and his nose ran, but he kept the mixture down.

Bill slowly opened his mouth to show the colossus standing in front of him that the egg was now in his stomach.

"Ya know kid, I didn't think you had a prayer, but you won 'er fair and square." The big guy then instructed the waiter to hand over the winnings to Billy.

"Thank you sir," Billy rasped, as a piece of egg shell caught in his throat.

"Have you done this before?" the over grown hayseed half-growled, starting to get some kind of an inkling that he'd been had.

"N-no sir!" Billy smiled, like a cub scout at his first pack circle.

Eddie saw what might be coming and pulled a two dollar bill from his wallet. He handed it to the waiter and broadcast in a booming voice, "Several rounds for our good friends at the corner table and take a one for yourself."

This seemed to oil the waters and the bear-like looser sat down with his buddies. Meanwhile, Bill and Eddie inched their way towards the door, opened it quickly and sprinted for the Bug. They didn't want to take any chances with the barrel lifting champions from Upper Yuca County. Ed slammed the Beetle into first and laid a respectful line of rubber along the asphalt that led out of Mary Hill.

*

Five minutes later Billy yelled, "Stop the car!"

Eddie came to a screeching halt and was amazed to see William Francis make a rocket powered exit from the Volks. Teddy Carlsen had held things in place as long as possible and now free of the Volks, he had a major discussion with Earl at the end of a make believe white telephone.

Still spitting egg shells, Bill got back into the Bug and heaved a ragged sigh, "I'll never try that one again Eddie."

"Why not Billy? The way I score it, we're up by eight bucks."

"What do you mean by we Kimosabi," Billy kidded his best pal. *I think that's how Jay Silverheels would have handled things.* On the serious side, the egg eating expert from the S.A.C fully intended to pass a pair of deuces Ed's way.

139

27

Eddie promised that the term egghead would be a private joke between Billy and himself. Young Master Carlsen was okay with that because, number one, he had plenty of nicknames and number two, he really wanted to leave the egg-out, or maybe it was egg-up in the outer regions of his fuzzy recollection, deep dark—Jeez, I'd like to forget that one—misty memory bank.

*

Friday of the following week Billy was trying to choke down an overflowing bowl of silage salad at Barfman when Donna plunked her cute behind onto the chair opposite the chicken kid—another label that Ed had sworn never to use.

"Miss Parker of the Port," Billy half-gagged, before swallowing a king-sized chuck of rabbit food.

"Hi Billy!" Donna flashed a smile that would've melted an iceberg.

"So what's up Doc?" Bill had placed his upper teeth over his lower lip in an attempt to look like Bugs Bunny.

"You've been eating too many carrots Teddy," Donna giggled.

"Nope, they only use spinach in this garden delight."

"Yeah, but the vinegar, mixed with used motor oil kind of defines it."

"I take it, as one of Flora's star performers, you've been trusted with the secret recipe for the dressing."

"But of course darling," Donna vamped, while batting her eyelashes.

"So what's new Greta, or do you *vant* to be alone?"

"That's really why I *vanted* to talk you Billy. I most certainly don't *vant* to be alone," she harsh whispered in a passable imitation of the great Garbo. "How'd you like to go with me to a party at the Vatican tomorrow night."

Sowsbury boasted a large Italian community and the centre piece of the predominantly Catholic south end was St. Mary's Cathedral.

Four, year sixty-five Aggies enrolled in the Agricultural Economics option, had rented a two-story, five bedroom house that was on the same street as St. Mary's. For obvious reasons it was called the Vatican. William Francis had been to the Bear Flag and now he was being presented with a gold plated invitation to visit the Vatican—without the Sistine Chapel of course.

"You're on babe!" Billy charmed.

"All right then Teddy, pick me up at Udderson Hall around seven-thirty."

"Not ta worry little missy, Irving and I'll be there pronto like." Billy figured the Duke might have said something like that.

"You've been watching too many movies Billy," Donna chuckled.

"Just part of the Carlsen charisma." Billy clasped his hands behind neck while tilting on his chair. "Anon, anon sweet Princes, or happy trails to you until we meet again."

"Dale and Buttermilk, right?"

"More like Lorne Greene and Roy Rogers wouldn't you say, my dark haired beauty."

"Later Billy." Donna threw a wave over her shoulder, before heading towards the exit sign.

*

It was a red bricked, three story, solidly built vintage home, featuring a white pillared, roofed porch. A wide staircase led to a mammoth, oak front door centrepieced by a brass plated pull chime. The Vatican wasn't exactly a rival for the real thing in Rome, but it did have a certain flair and was typical of the century dwellings that were lined up like Picadilly Commandos along this first settled Sowsbury street.

Mike Brown, sporting a crew cut and wire glasses, met them at the door. He was five-eight and wheat shaft thin. The four-eyed Junior was also a real character. As soon as he spotted Donna Mike broke into a "Ted Mack Amateur Hour" rendition of the Ritchie Valens hit; "Oh Donna, oh Donna," his sour notes curdling the air.

I'll betcha, Ritchie, Buddy and the Big Bopper are turning over in their graves listening to that one Billy thought to himself.

"Mike, you're the ace of spades in my deck," Donna chuckled, before giving him a peck on the cheek. "and I'd like you to meet Bill Carlsen."

"Hey Mike, how's it goin' ?" Billy grinned, while shaking hands.

"Did you play rugger in the fall?" Mike asked, as he led them from the hallway into a spacious living room. He had to shout to be heard over, "I Saw Her Standing There" blasting full throttle from a Clairtone Hi-Fi.

"Yeah, I was the scrum-half. Do you know Taffy Morgan?" Bill raised his voice.

"Sure do. Taffy's an old drinking buddy from way back."

This seemed to break the ice and from that point on Billy was accepted as an equal, even though he was just a lowly Frosh. William Francis was then introduced to the other keepers of the Vatican, George Clark, Jack Darling and Sid Thompson. Again the fact that Billy was well acquainted with people like Charlie Ross and Gary Barker smoothed out the speed bumps.

"So, would you like a beer Carlsen?" Mike offered, while showing Billy the way to the kitchen. Donna was talking to several of her classmates and Bill had gone with Mike to get refreshments.

"A beer would be great and a glass of wine for Donna."

"The wine's on the kitchen table and the beer's in an old Kelvinator in the pantry," Mike informed Billy, while pointing to a door at the end of the room.

William Francis poured out a glass of Chateau Gai medium dry red then went into the pantry. The fridge was full of stubbies but the beer bottles had no labels.

"Hey, what kind of brew is this?" Billy asked, looking around for a church key.

"Vatican Pale Ale," Mike said with a straight face.

"Oh, I get it, bathtub hooch right?"

"Aye boyo, as Taffy would say."

"Well isn't that somethin', I've always wanted to give homebrewing a try, but I'm at Hereford and there's no way."

"Right you are there Billy. If old Abra-Dean Angus ever found out, you'd be up cow pie creek without a barge pole."

Billy was curious about the process and Mike filled him in on how to make the do-it-yourself barley sandwiches. The thing that intrigued Young Master Carlsen the most, was the cost per bottle. It worked out to be about one shinny Canadian copper.

The beer was like ambrosia from on high, the potato chips, peanuts, popcorn and pepperoni were a feast to be savoured and the jokes, dancing and music kept the party animals amused all night long. Well past midnight Billy and Donna thanked their hosts and departed the Vatican. Donna had some heavy duty scabbing to do for a Monday practical in dress making, so much to his chagrin, Teddy received a quick good night kiss and was sent on his way without the highly anticipated game of touch football, and other body parts, in Irving's spacious back seat.

28

"You got it right Eddie, you can buy a beer kit from the IGA, at least that's what Mike Brown told me."

"Now let me get this straight Billy, with all the expenses involved the price per bottle is just about one red cent."

"Yep, I figured it out. Each kit makes five gallons of brew and that'll give us almost seventy bottles."

"So Billy, the kit's about seventy cents right, but what about the sugar?"

"Well actually sixty-five, and no sweat with the sugar, we can liberate that from Barfman."

"How about the capper and caps?" Ed frowned.

"Mike said they got a bushel of them free from a a local source. He'll pass along the caps and lend us their capper."

"Sounds like you might be on to something there Carlsen. I have three squares of empties in my closet. That works out to 72 stubbies."

"The real good news my fine feathered friend is; by bootlegging the beer in Hereford for two-bits a pop we could clear around sixteen bucks." Bill rubbed his hands like a well practiced moneylender.

"Hey, you did that without a slide rule Billy. Boy, eight smackaroos each would buy a lot of gas."

"Precisely what I was thinking Sudsie Samson, resident brewmaster of the third. Has a nice ring to it eh?"

There were other hurtles to overcome, but since it was a quiet Sunday morning, and all the administrative staff were enjoying their weekend, no one noticed that a clean, plastic garbage can had disappeared from a hallway outside the main office. On Monday afternoon during their scheduled Chemistry Lab. Eddie stuffed a length of rubber tubing into his brief case along with a metal 'H' clamp—this would act as a siphon and tap. They needed cheese cloth to cover the top of the garbage can that would contain the magic elixir, but this ceased to be a major difficulty when Donna loaned Billy a pair of her pantyhose.

Tuesday after classes Bill and Ed drove to the IGA and purchased a beer kit. It took them until the end of the week to put together enough sugar, but by Saturday morning it was time for great fermentations. They added the contents of the kit to the boosted wort, poured in five gallons of water, dumped in the sucrose and finally sprinkled a package of brewers yeast on top of the foamy mixture. With Donna's contribution fitted over the top, the sloshing container was placed carefully in the back of Eddie's closet—pants shirts and coats hiding it from prying eyes.

Mike had also confided in Billy that you really didn't need a fancy hydrometer to measure the specific gravity of the suds. It was far easier just to wait until no bubbles appeared on the surface of the liquid and then do your bottling. He also told them that you needed to add sugar to the mix before you bottled, so it would undergo a secondary fermentation in order to carbonate the beer in the stubbies.

*

Three weeks later, the lager twins had gathered in the privacy of Ed's room to bottle the golden nectar.

"Are you sure about the amount of sugar?"

"Sure as shootin' Eddie. Mike said a cup of sugar and that's all there is to it."

"Seems like a lot Billy."

"Well, it can't hurt because the stuff's flatter than a prairie stubble field. Not a bubble in two days. I figure that any extra will produce a little more alcohol when things are all finished. Stronger beer's okay in my books."

"Jeepers creepers Mr. Peepers, we've got it made in the shade. You work the capper and I'll fill the bottles."

They siphoned and capped like a well rehearsed pit crew. One hour later all the brownies were topped up with sweetest brew this side of a Carling's malt shop. Ed had put up with the big plastic can for twenty-one days and wanted to get things back to normal in his digs, so he asked Billy to stash the three two-fours, that were almost full, in the closet that Bill shared with Pete in 301.

William Francis figured that the squares, in amongst the parkas, pacs and mitts, wouldn't be a problem because he could cover up the cases with a laundry bag and a pile of old clothes. Good Aggie Eastman would be none the wiser.

*

Several nights later Billy was at his desk writing up a Physics Lab. report. Pete was over at the library on a study date with Tova. Pretty exciting stuff eh? Well maybe they got to hold hands, or smooch in the stacks.

Bill had started to yawn and was considering calling it a night when all hell broke loose. It sounded like a bunch of firecrackers, on the twenty-fourth of May, were being let off behind the wooden door of the closet. Billy jumped to his feet and yanked on the closet door handle. He was horrified to see a blanket of white, creeping foam flowing like a miniature tidal wave across the tiled floor. The beer bottles had burst open and the place smelt like a brewery.

Eddie was out on a date with Alice, so Terrible Teddy was front and centre when it came to the clean up committee. Bill knew there was a janitor's storeroom at the end of the hall. Using his thin, plastic Aggie ID card he slipped the lock and hauled out a mop and squeeze bucket. Working like a trooper Billy sopped up the suds and filled the bucket. The well used galvanized container, sporting a squeeze handle attachment, was mounted on a squeaky set of rust ridden casters, so he was able to roll it to the showers and dump the contents down the drain. He filled the bucket with fresh water and managed to clean up the mess before Pete got back. The broken beer bottles and soaked cases were put into green garbage bags. Bill, constantly looking over his shoulder, carted these to a dumpster that was located near the parking lot entrance of Hereford. Luckily no one was around and he didn't have to answer any questions.

*

"Jeez Carlsen, this place smells like a beer hall,"Pete wrinkled his nose, as he entered the room. "If a proctor walked in right now we'd both be in deep doo-doo."

146

"Okay Sherlock you got me. Eddie gave me a bottle of Dow ale and I was about halfway through when I accidently elbowed the sucker. Then it was slam-bam-thank you-ma'am, all over my desk and lab report."

"The wages of sin Carlsen," Pete guppy-gulped several times, before starting to cry.

"Hey Eastman, it was only a beer and you don't even like beer. Lighten up eh?"

"I-It's not the beer you dork," Pete chocked out the words. "Tova and I had a big fight and we've busted up."

"Sorry Pete that's a tough one," Bill sympathized. He really liked his roomie and hated to see him blubbering away like the winner of an onion peeling contest.

"It was so stupid Billy. She asked if I liked her hair short or long. I said that long would likely suit her better. Since she has it cut short this was the wrong thing to say. One gaffe led to another and I got angry too and swore at her."

"Not a wise move, I would hazard a guess."

"Holy jumpin' catfish Billy, I just said; I don't really see why in hell you're making such a big deal out of your God damned hair. Taking the Lord's name in vain was the last straw, and she stomped out of Yorkshire saying she never wanted to see me again."

"Hang tough Eastman, I'll betcha in a day or two she'll have settled down and you'll be able to smooth things out."

Pete thought it over for a minute, then gave a thin smile. "You're probably right but right now, I just want to go lights out. I'm not used to all this emotional stuff."

The next day Bill explained to Eddie what had happened to the homebrew contract. They must have added the wrong amount of sugar and the pressure build up of carbon dioxide was just too much for the beer bottles to handle. Pop, pop, fizz, fizz was the end result. Ed was disappointed but figured they'd given it a try and maybe, just maybe, they weren't cut out be bootleggers. If Floor Fink Guardwell had caught them in their suds for sale operation, it would likely have meant a one-way out of Hereford.

"Sleeping dogs Billy," were Eddie's final words on the subject.

*

When Bill ran into Mike Brown at Barfman, later in the week, he asked about the addition of sugar to the flat beer.

"Just like I told you Carlsen. You add two tablespoons of sugar to one cup of water and dump it into the mix."

"Holy mackinaw!" Billy moaned. "I've really got to start writing some of this stuff down."

148

29

Billy wanted to play hockey, but he wasn't good enough to make the Varsity. The obvious solution? Become a 'house leaguer'. His year had iced four teams in the Frosh intra-murals and William Francis patrolled the blueline for the "Third Floor Dragons." The first game of the season pitted them against Hereford's "Second Floor Tigers."

He'd brought his dad's wartime duffel bag stuffed full of shin pads, pants, gloves, shoulder pads, elbow pads, jock strap—with cup, Leafs sweater, socks, friction tape, a pair of braces and a garter belt. No, he wasn't a transvestite, this is what real men wore to keep their hockey socks from bunching about the ankles. Skates and a curved stick rounded out the equipment list. He'd been magnificently turned out thanks to several judicious acquisitions at Canada Tire. Since Billy worked there in his senior year, the lucky stiff had received a five percent discount on all items purchased. Old man Montroy—the local majordomo of an empire that printed money more valuable than the Canadian dollar—really did have a generous heart. He only looked a little bit like Ebeniser Scrooge. Those brass plated ball points given to the part-timers at Christmas were always the highlight of the yuletide. Where else could you get a magic pen that would turn a dull, mossy green all by itself before Easter.

*

In the dressing room, moments before the Saturday night match-up at the Phys. Ed. rink, Billy, Pete and Eddie dressed confidently.

"These bums from the second couldn't punch their way out of a wet pair of panties," Eddie pontificated loudly.

"Friggin' A," Pete shouted, as he laced up his skates.

"H-Holy cow, that's the second time you've said the 'F' word since I've known you," Bill sputtered, amazed at the intensity of the moment.

"Carry that on to the ice Eastman," Eddie whooped, as the gladiators from the third got up to do battle.

It was a woodchoppers ball. The Tigers were all elbows, slashes, spears and high sticks. They must have ridden with the Calvary because charging seemed to be the only check they knew. Billy was lucky enough to score the first goal late in the opening period, but after the puck crossed the goal line he was leveled by Moose Manders. Hiram Percy Manders, the self appointed enforcer of the second floor skaters, was six-two and tipped the scales at two-thirty-five. Bill got up starry-eyed after the late hit but smiled winningly, as he baited the Tigers Policeman. "That's a score Percy or maybe you'd like me to spell that for you as in one zip eh?"

"Watch your mouth Carlsen we've still got two to play."

The Tigers tallied in the second but halfway through the third, Eddie took a beakaway pass from Pete, inches from the blueline, roared in on the goalie and lifted a perfect backhand into the net. Just as Rocket Samson emerged from behind the cage, hands raised, Moose Manders landed a vicious two hander on the back of Eddie's legs.

Edward H. hit the deck faster than a hooker wearing hinged heels at a Breeder's Convention. Manders skated to centre ice, a big smirk plastered all over his Porky Pig face. Billy went ballistic. After dropping his gloves, he made a beeline for the Moose. The king-sized bully turned to meet William Francis head on and skated towards Bill, arms open, ready to enfold his opponent in a crushing bear hug. This was a standard tactic for the lumbering colossus who was a member of the College wrestling team. He'd grab his victim, throw him to the ice and get in several haymakers before the linesmen broke it up. Billy realized he only had one chance and used his momentum, plus that of the onrushing eighteen wheeler, to deliver a right upper cut to the solar plexus of the attacking giant. An image of David and Goliath flashed across Billy's mind as Moose banged over backwards and hit his head hard on the ice. Manders was carried off and never returned. The Dragons reigned victorious. After the game several cars, loaded with happy puck merchants, roared to the Empire to celebrate their team's first league win.

"Boy you sure showed that overgrown sack of chicken guts a thing of two," Eddie trumpeted after they'd been served.

"Yeah, and did you see the way Manders looked when he tried to get up? He was completely out of it and didn't know his ass from a hole in the ground," Pete guffawed.

This was the first time that good Aggie Eastman had been to the pub and Billy was extremely nervous because the magic birth certificate only worked for one out of two.

"I-It may not be over yet," William Francis croaked, as he spotted Moose entering the men's beverage room.

The hulking, hockey hotshot marched directly to their table. Towering over Billy, Manders was grinning coast to coast. *Oh, oh Batman and the Joker.*

"Put her there Carlsen. You're all right, I've won most of 'em but you beat me fair and square."

Billy reached out for the large calloused hand and shook it cautiously. He'd been sucker punched in the past and had his guard up. Nothing happened and several seconds later he was released from the iron grip. Moose left the table before anyone could speak. The three Dragons sat there open mouthed and silent.

"Maybe that knock on the noggin made him a little punch drunk," Eddie whispered cautiously, breaking the hush that had come over the group.

"By golly, I thought he was going to clean your clock Billy," Pete exhaled noisily, as he watched Moose join a group of his buddies.

"Me too!" Billy nodded. "Just like Ajax the Foaming Cleanser, budda-dubba-doop, right down the old dirt shoot."

"I think that might have been drain," Eddie corrected.

"Whatever! It was still a close one."

"Yep, but the Dargons got their first 'W' and for sure; we won't get skunked this season," Pete burbled happily.

Pete and Tova, following the collateral damage from their lover's quarrel, were now Splitsville. Peter Martin Eastman was presently unattached and sampling the forbidden fruit denied to him by his strict Baptist upbringing.

The beer he was belting back, as if it were a glass of milk, was the second of his life. The Good Aggie had a sudden flash and pictured himself in a new light. He was James Dean, a rebel with a cause, or something like that. Marlon Brando riding his Harley into a quiet town—hell bent for action.

"Bring on the dancing girls," Pete muttered incoherently, as they ordered another round.

"What's that?" Eddie shouted, over the din of the raucous beverage room.

"N-Nothing," Pete peeped meekly, before taking another large gulp of ale.

*

Several minutes later, Eddie excused himself saying he was going over to Alice's place. Pete and Bill decided to stay for a couple more, and settled back to watch the final minutes of "Hockey Night In Canada" that was being shown on the Pub's snowy Sylvania. To their amazement the lowly Boston Bruins were clobbering the Leafs eleven to one. When the game was over Billy suggested they take a walk through the Ladies and Escorts.

"Okay Carlsen, but you know this beer must be half-water because I can't feel a thing."

When Pete got to his feet he was shocked to find that the room had been placed on a merry-go-round. He thumped back down, wondering why his legs wouldn't propel him forward. Bill caught Pete the second time he tried for the vertical and prevented him from knocking over the table.

"Come on Eastman, it's time to hit the trail, we'll save the L&E for another night."

*

The cold air nailed Pete harder than the *Titanic* ramming an iceberg. He began to sway back and forth like an old growth pine being pushed around by gale force winds. Billy steadied Pete from behind and with a great deal of effort, guided him into the back seat of the Chevy.

"Gee whiz, maybe there was something in that brew," Pete groaned loudly, as they drove back to Hereford.

152

The next evening Pete, wanting to patch things up, gave Tova a call and confessed his sins. He promised her that he would never touch another drop, would clean up his language, would never swear or raise his voice in anger again and would remain true forever. Tova listened quietly as her boyfriend poured out his heart. After he'd finished, his well rehearsed speech, she granted Pete forgiveness, and promised to bake him a batch of chocolate chip cookies. LOVE CONQUERS ALL EH?

30

Donna had been up to her delightful rear end in alligators and delicious side dishes at the Hogstroff Hall cafeteria for two weeks. It turned out to be a dry spell for Billy because Donna along with the other girls in '65, taking a course in Nutrition, had been given the responsibility of planning, preparing and serving all the meals for the last part of February. It was a hands on practical. Their performance, or lack thereof, would mean a make it or break it in the subject. Donna dispalyed exceptional skill as the dinning room supervisor, and when the final marks were posted she was awarded one of the highest grades ever. Flora—the Kate Aitken of Sowsbury—had granted her a 95 in Institutional Management.

*

"Congratulations!" Billy smiled approvingly, as Donna took a seat opposite him in Barthman on the 29th day of the shortest month. The drought was over.

"I guess there aren't any secrets around here," she said, a hint of anger in her voice.

"Talked to Alice yesterday and I'm afraid she spilled the beans."

"Alice should have kept her big mouth shut, but I think she meant well."

"Cool it babe, it's kinda like scoring fifty in the NHL. You and the Rocket eh?"

"Well let's forget that Billy. Life can be too much of; what have you done for me lately, so ancient history all right?"

"Fine by me Donna."

"Okay Teddy, now we've got that one straight, are you trying out for Curtain Crashers?"

"Curtain what?"

"It's a stage production, written and produced by the students of Hay Seed U," Donna stated seriously.

"Hey, that sounds like a real blast," Billy enthused, picturing himself as a budding Bruno Gerussi.

"You know, the greatest thing about being involved in 'Crashers' are the parties at the Empire after rehearsals."

"Where do I sign up?" Billy beamed.

"I'm doing some of the work on costumes, so I'll mention your name to Ted Grant. He's the stage director this year."

"I did a couple of plays when I was in high school, and I'd love to be in this Curtain thing."

"And, what have you been up to Billy?" she asked, a loaded gun smoking in her hand. "I hear via the grapevine, you were at the St. Alfred's dance."

"Yeah, strictly out of boredom. Boy, when you get to see those bimbo nurses, you realize how good we've got it here on campus," William Francis fibbed smoothly.

Donna chuckled before saying, "A refrigerator salesman on Baffin Island may turn out to be your true calling Teddy." They finished their lunch, then left Barthman. Afternoon lectures and labs would begin at one-thirty.

Bill made his college stage debut as a horse's ass. Some suspected this of him already, but Curtain Crashers merely confirmed this less than kind judgement. The skit involved a bending of the Lady Godiva tale and the continuation of the story involving an after the ride incident. Sir Harry Mufdiva—you can see it's getting weird from the get go—was not too pleased by his wife's performance and is about to send her to a nunnery. The famous bare naked Lady just happens to look a lot like Charlie Ross in drag and "she" asserts herself by banging the astonished Lord over the head with a water pail—no this is not Jack and Jill. Now enter the horse who's in love with the long haired beauty. Good old Trigger—the faithful beast of burden not the campus cop—sits triumphantly on the sprawled nobleman and is hugged fervently by her Ladyship. The curtain of course crashes ending the scene.

Eddie stared as the front of the horse and, you guessed it, William Francis was the rear end. The audience loved it and Charlie was reported in the College Review as the most promising starlet of the year.

It was whispered in certain circles that an Academy Award was just over the blue horizon for him/her. The final after the show party at the Empire turned out to be a real barn burner.

*

"Charlie you were great," Donna giggled. "you've defined Lady Godiva forever."

"Yeah, Elizabeth Taylor was supposed to get the part, but I had a better screen test," Charlie snorted.

"Really! I didn't know Liz tried out," Eddie exhaled loudly, looking disappointed. He'd consumed a tanker load of ale and was losing his grip on the moment.

"Relax Samson, you can still get to see her at the movies."

"Hey, good thinking Billy. Boy, do I ever need to visit the facilities," Eddie mumbled, before getting up from the table.

"You know I thought you made a perfect hind quarters," Alice purred softly, as she patted William Francis on the arm.

"Well here's looking at you kid." Billy raised his beer glass to eye level—eat your heart out Bogie.

"I thought you might have crushed the poor guy who played Sir Harry," Sandi Coulter said, before putting her arm around Charlie.

"That was my roomie and he's okay. Pete may not look it but he pumps a lot of iron and has abs of steel."

This got Alice's interest because she loved hunks and looking to see that Eddie was still in the washroom she cooed, "Does he have a girlfriend?"

"Yeah, big time!" Donna cut in. "You wouldn't want to tangle with Tova. She's nice, but I can picture her as a real Brunhilde. Tread lightly would be my advice."

Several minutes later Tom Grant got to his feet. Shouting over the din, he thanked the gathered throng for the best Curtain Crashers ever and invited everyone to come out again next year. It was getting near the closing time at the Empire, and Tom wished all those present a safe drive home. The lights blinked several times, the suds slingers began to clear the tables, and shortly thereafter the hall was empty.

Billy parked in a quiet spot behind the water tower. He'd been told by Eddie that this was the last place that Trigger was likely to check on his rounds. The tower was located on a high point and the cruiser would be approaching from downhill. It was therefore a no-brainer that lights on the windshield would be a signal to straighten up and fly right, giving the average Aggie enough time to get the hood up and start looking for engine problems.

*

"That was a great party and I'm sure glad you told me about Crashers," Billy sighed pleasurably, after placing his arm around Donna.

All you could hear in the car was the Rice Krispies-like, snap, crackle, and pop as the engine cooled. Donna rested her head on Bill's shoulder but she seemed tense.

"I thought you'd get a kick out it. The after rehearsal study sessions and tonight's cast blast were a lot of fun."

Billy really liked Donna—Ellen now out of reach—and hoped that someday soon, she might wear his class ring. He'd thought it over and knew that she'd also be the perfect partner for the big soiree in March. *What the hell, why not ask her now.* "Hey Donna, the Formal's coming up soon, and I was kinda hoping you'd go with me."

The Formal was Sowsburys gala event of the year. It was held at the end of College Fair days—tuxedos, long gowns and a real live orchestra. He figured that the lovely Miss Parker was a shoe-in as his main squeeze for the annual Prom. Donna had been voted by her year as their representative for Sow U's "Queen of the Ball" and King William the First was blossoming into a living color, BMOC trip, in his callow mind.

"I'd really love to Teddy, but Larry Dawgleish asked me last week and I said yes."

"Jeez, Donna, I thought we had something going. So what if this Clap College dog droppings guy can toss a football fifty yards. Big deal!" he grumbled.

"Now don't be that way. It's not because Larry's the quarterback of the Woodchucks and owns a new Mustang."

157

Donna was little ticked at having to defend herself but she continued in a calm voice, "His father just happens to run the most successful Vet. practice in the Province but that's not why I'm starting to date Lawrence. Doggie Dawgleish is very sincere and has a wonderful personality."

William Francis knew it was over and decided to be gracious. What the hell these guys from the V.D.C. could make a pile of cash in the real world, especially if they went into small animals. Gosh, who wouldn't be happy to take care of some wealthy babes cat. As far as that goes, maybe even her pet kitten. Yep, Billy had to admit, old Larry was destined to become a real pussy pleaser.

It was the last minute of game seven and we're down five to one, so why pull the goalie. "Well, I hope you and the pooch prick will live happily ever after," he harrumphed vindictively. Parting is such sweet sorrow.

31

Billy spent several woe-is-me days at the end of lonely street but soon recovered. One fine snowy morning, shortly thereafter, he ran into Gary Barker at the coffee shop and they got to talking about their plans after the Aggie degree was finally pinned on the wall. Gary wanted to be a Civil Engineer, and said that he was thinking of transferring to McMaster next year to complete the requirements for a Bachelor of Applied Science and the coveted iron ring.

"So how about you Carlsen?"

"Beats me for sure, but I'd kinda like to give teaching a shot."

"If you're serious Billy, then call the school board and tell them you're available as a supply."

"You mean they'd hire a Frosh to mind the rug rats for a day?"

"First of all, don't let on that you're in first year and ask for high school not elementary."

"Gosh, I don't know if I could handle that one."

"No sweat, I filled in last winter and got twenty-four bucks for eight hours on the job. I was thinking the same thing as you, but one day in the trenches convinced me I wasn't cut out to be a nursemaid to a bunch of snot nosed teenagers."

"Ha-Have you still got the number to call?" Bill asked eagerly, seeing the dollar signs roll by like symbols on a slot-machine. Three greenbacks an hour was big money where he came from.

"Look in Ma Bell's bible. It'll be there under the Sowsbury and District School Board."

"Hey, thanks Gary, that's another one I owe you."

"Yeah, a couple of quarts would go down real good some night at Young Peoples, gotta fly Billy, Biochem. at eleven eh?"

*

The next day, right after lunch, Bill called the Board of Education office located on Edward Street.

Yes, they did hire Cow U students to do supply work and the secretary, who answered the call, would put his name on a list. Billy heard nothing for a week and was surprized when Eddie rapped on his door shortly after supper one evening, informing him that some broad with a real sexy voice was on the phone wanting to talk to William Carlsen.

"Hello," Billy said, his voice exuding confidence.

"Mr. Carlsen?"

"The one and only," he answered, playing Mr. Smartass.

"Miss Payne of the school board calling. You're on our supply roster and we'd like you to fill in for Mr. Everett at Fowler Collegiate tomorrow."

Bill did a rapid run down of his classes for the next day and figured that ditching wouldn't be a major difficulty. "No problem ma'am, what time would you like me to be there?"

"Eight o'clock sharp. You'll receive your instructions and lesson plans from Mr. McBride the school's Vice-Principal."

"Sin city eh?"

"What did you say Mr. Carlsen?"

"A Principal in charge of vice, just a little humour ma'am."

"If you want this assignment, I'd suggest you keep your smutty jokes to yourself."

"Sorry, I'll remember that and be on deck first thing tomorrow."

"Very well," Miss Payne-In-The-Ass fumed, slamming her black handled phone onto its squat rotary cradle.

*

Billy didn't sleep well. He tossed and turned, mentally rehearsing a dozen challenging encounters with keen, eager minds—Mr. Chips, move over eh? Red-eyed and dry-mouthed, William Francis Carlsen, a long shot candidate for a Bachelor of Science in Agriculture, tumbled into Irving at 7:30 the next morning and set sail for Fowler High.

It was a classic red bricked structure, right out of the early thirties. There was even an etched-in-stone sign over the west door that read 'Boys Entrance' and a similar engraving on the east door identifying it as the 'Girls Entrance'.

160

The finely chiseled letters were from a long gone era and both sexes now entered the hallowed halls of old Fowler wherever they pleased. Bill found the office with little difficulty and met Mr. McBride. He was then handed a letter sized folder by the kindly man who ran hookers and crap tables. The short, rolly polly Vice-Principal suggested that the men's staff room might be a good place to review the assigned teaching duties. Billy sat in a corner by himself and poured over the detailed lesson plans that had been provided by Mr. Everett. No one in the room spoke to him. After all, he was only a supply, and who in the hell gave a damn about some wet-behind-the-ears college kid they'd never see again.

The first period of the day was Grade 10 Science and Bill did his best to demonstrate the mysteries of the compound microscope. He gave out a set of plant cell slides and told the class to make detailed diagrams of what they observed.

"What are these green things sir?" A well endowed sixteen year old girl asked, while Bill viewed the plant world under high resolution. She was pressing a firm round breast into his back as she attempted to peer over his shoulder. Billy was acutely aware of her physical presence and the disturbing augmentation occurring south of his belt buckle.

"Th-There chloroplasts," he squeaked, fighting to control his growing concern. Bill was wearing a white lab. coat and very carefully, hands-in-pockets, moved around the buxom beauty in order to make his way to the front demonstration bench.

The forty minute class went by quickly, after his initial brush with an unexpected side of the teaching profession. At 9:40, Teddy the Teacher welcomed a grade 9 class who spent a period mutilating a pail full of crayfish, fresh from a dip in 40% formaldehyde. The fancy term was dissection, but the flashing scalpels, tweezers and probes wielded by the chattering munchkins was enough to make Jack the Ripper look like a skilled surgeon. The third period of the morning turned out to be a repeat of the plant cell extravaganza. This time, Billy carefully avoided close contact of the first kind.

Lunch was next and William Francis dined on a rubbery hog dog smothered in mustard and ketchup. He sat alone in a quiet corner of the staff cafeteria pondering the instructions he'd been given for the afternoon classes.

"Mind if I sit here?" A great bear of man rumbled, just as Bill pushed his chair back.

"Be my guest sir," Billy gulped.

"Ross Bradley!" The burly, bespectacled, dark haired hulk smiled, extending a ham like hand.

"Pleased to meet you sir," Billy replied timidly, his fingers tingling from the bone-crushing grip.

"I'm the Head of the Science Department and you're the supply for Everett right?"

"Yes sir, I just did his first three classes."

"Well, you must've done something right. My room's directly across from Everett's and I didn't hear anything, other than normal classroom chatter, coming from the your side of the hall. Please call me Ross."

"Y-Yes sir, Ross," Billy stammered

"That's better, you got it fifty percent right."

"Sorry Ross, I'm so used to the sir bit from the College that it's automatic."

"I see by the note I found in my mailbox this morning that your name's William Carlsen," Ross spoke in a friendly manner, trying his best to make Billy feel a part of things

"Right on Mr.Bradley, I-I mean, sir, uh Ross."

"So you want to be a teacher after you graduate eh?"

"I'm considering it. From what I've seen today it might be okay."

"Yes, it's an interesting job and we're short of good staff these days. If you're still serious when that Aggie degree's in your back pocket, give me a call and we might be able to do a little business."

"Gee, thanks sir, I've gotta run now for a lunch room supervision. It's been swell meeting you."

"Good luck with pig pen patrol," Ross quipped, before giving a friendly good-bye wave.

Pig pen, I wonder why he said that? Bill mused as he made his way to the student cafeteria. By the end of the second lunch period when the starving boys and girls of Fowler had hoovered up a boxcar full of fires and gravy, bags of chips, chocolate bars and bucket loads of licorice sticks he knew what Mr. Bradley was talking about. The trays left behind, full of garbage, were mute testimony to the ravenous horde of two legged locusts that had ravaged the dinning hall.

*

The afternoon started off with Senior Chemistry. The students were to perform an experiment dealing with the effect of temperature on the rate of a chemical reaction, or "the hotter she gets the faster she goes." The class of twenty-four had been divided into twelve working groups. Further split into four teams, they would test the reacting solutions at several different temperatures: zero Celsius, ten Celsius, room temperature and thirty Celsius.

There was ice available to lower the temperature of the water baths into which the test tubes containing the reacting solutions would be placed, and hot plates to get things above room temperature. Three, one litre beakers, acting as water baths, had been on the side counter since the previous day, these were obviously at room temperature. The reaction involved starch combining with iodine which produced a deep purple colour when the chemical change was complete. The students, using stop watches, timed the reacting solutions from the point of mixing until a purple pigment appeared.

Once the experiment was underway, Bill circulated around the room trying to be of assistance. The second group he approached seemed to be having trouble as they added ice, removed ice then tried to warm up the water bath on a hot plate.

"Which group are you?" Billy asked.

"Well sir," one of the boys answered brightly. "we're trying to get this puppy to room temperature."

Bill straight-faced, resisting the urge to assail the airwaves with gales of uproarious laughter. "In that case carry on!"

163

Billy spotted another twosome who were having problems and went over to help.

"Sir, we can't get this dumb thermometer to give us proper readings," a buxom brunette griped.

"Ladies," William Francis informed them, as politely as possible. "perhaps it would work better if you took it out of its plastic storage tube."

"Gee, thanks Mr. Carlsen," the blonde member of the dynamic duo gushed, as she removed the red liquid thermometer from its clear, colourless casing.

*

During the post lab. discussion one of the boys in the class asked why they had to use Celsius instead of Fahrenheit, which everyone was familiar with.

"It's the standard system used by scientists to communicate data all over the world. A chemist in Paris can share his findings with someone in Toronto and they'd both be on the same page," Bill explained patiently.

"That's crap sir, those guys in Paris are a bunch of arrogant homers and wouldn't share a bread crumb with a canary."

Billy grinned. "Easy now, I was across the pond last summer and the French are okay, but rest assured, Canada will never go metric because it would cost too much and our friends south of the border sure won't convert. It'd be really stupid to have a different system of units than your major trading partner."

"Right on Mr. Carlsen," the big senior shouted before he sat down.

When all the results had been tabulated it appeared that at higher temperatures it took less time for the deep purple to appear, proving once and for all; the hotter she is the faster she goes.

*

Bill's next assignment was an on-call, which meant he had to cover a class for a teacher who was on a field trip. Billy finished the day with a repeat of period one and another attempt at verifying the basic principles of Chemistry.

William Francis taught six classes, managed to have lunch, survived pig pen patrol and played baby-sitter for some English expert who'd taken his senior class to a special showing of "Hamlet" at the Roxy. Bill stayed in Mr. Everett's homeroom until four-thirty, helping two very friendly female students who were struggling with the mysteries of Gas Law problems. Mr. Boyle and his partner in crime Mr. Charles were often difficult dudes to deal with.

*

Billy, feeling the effects of the whirlwind day, walked slowly across the staff parking lot, and was hunting for his car keys when Ross Bradley approached the side of the Bel Air.

"How goes it?" the friendly Department Head asked cheerfully.

"Well sir, you guys sure work hard for your money. I kinda feel like old Sylvester after a trip through the knothole, but I really liked it."

"The only things you haven't been exposed to are lesson planning, extracurricular duties, for instance I coached football this fall, and the marking we do at home, but that gets easier as time goes on."

"You mean you still have more to do in the evening?"

"It comes with the territory Mr. Carlsen but the summers make up for it, if you're not taking courses."

"I've got to get through three more years at Sowsbury, but I'd still like to give it a try."

"As I said before, give me a call when you graduate and by the way I'm '54 S.A.C."

"Hey, how about that, no wonder you're such a nice guy!" Bill grinned, while opening the door of his Chevy.

32

It came in like a lamb. The first one was sunny and spring warm. The steely grip of winter was letting go, and maybe the groundhog was right. On February the 2nd, according to the whispers of Sowsbury Sam, it would only be six more weeks. Considering the first day of the Vernal Equinox was on or about March 21, this wasn't exactly a foolish venture along the precarious reaches of a partially sawed limb.

Billy had been dumped by Donna, but there was a tiny spot of light in the far corners of his universe. Judy was Splitsville with her boyfriend and delivered this message to Bill one morning between classes. They had both arrived at the coffee shop on an hours respite before a pre-lunch lecture.

"Well, hello Billy," she bubbled, while picking up a butter tart.

"Hey Jude! Boy, that would make a great tile for a song."

"Yeah, pass that one on to John and Paul. You never know."

"So how's it going with the big heart throb back in the old hometown?"

She stared at him for a moment before he noticed a round, glistening tear slowly making its way towards her jaw line. "The rat fink called me on the weekend and broke things off because he's not sure I'm really the one."

"He must be a total dipstick. You're beautiful, intelligent and a real mean piece of ass," Billy inhaled deeeply, before holding his breath.

Judy was about to tell him to take a long walk on a short pier when she realized that, in a left handed way, she was being paid an honest compliment. To be considered, bright, attractive and desirable by a guy who wasn't handsome, but definitely in the cute category was a boost to her battered self esteem.

"Y-You have an odd way on putting things Teddy, but I'll take that as a positive," she replied hesitantly

"Absolutely Jude, you're a keeper in my books."

Judy was pleased by Billy's words and decided that a dab of sympathetic salve might help to restore their bygone magic. She sighed dramatically before saying, "I got it through the grapevine that Donna left you high and dry. She sure is missing the boat by dating Larry. He may be smart, but he's still an arrogant, spoiled rich kid."

This was a real ego trip for Billy, clearing his throat he croaked nervously, "Wouldja care to sit with me?"

Judy pretended to think it over for a moment, then cooed musically, "That'd be a pleasure Mr. Carlsen."

*

They talked about everything including old times. Twenty minutes later it seemed like they'd never been apart. Billy was riding a natural high and since they were both on the rebound he decided to take a chance.

"I know, you know by now, that I asked Donna to the Formal but she's smitten with Doctor Dog Lead, so I was wondering if....."

"I'd love to Billy!" she jumped in. "I got the news yesterday, that I've been elected by my year to be their representative in the Queen contest."

King William, arisen from the ashes. A regular uptight out of sight modern day Phoenix—*artsy fartsy eh?* Life's a washtub full of ice cold beer!

*

Rust Hog, seizing a moment of divine inspiration, was convinced that even a Yonge Street farmer could become a son of the land. He approached Billy the following day after class and asked him if he'd like to show a prize goat during College Fair days.

"Outta my league Doctor McTavish, I wouldn't know the front end from the business end," Bill lamented.

"Not to worry son, I've watched you in class and you seem to have a knack with all creatures great and small."

"Sounds like a wonderful title for a book sir."

"Yes, you're right Mr. Carlsen, maybe I should be writing instead of teaching."

167

"If I were you sir, I'd stick with the chalk and brush contract."

"Far more secure, I see your point. Now look here Carlsen, I'm serious, and being in the ring with a 'first in show' wouldn't hurt your chances for an honours grade."

The carrot had been dangled on the pole and William Francis suddenly saw the advantages of becoming an Animal Husbandry convert.

"Okay sir, I'm your man," Billy agreed, knowing that every mark he could beg, borrow or steal might be the secure anchor he needed to keep him from floating down river.

*

The "big shew", as Ed Sullivan would say, was held towards the end of College Fair and two days before the crowning of the campus Queen.

"Now take a firm grip on the halter and let him know who's boss once you're in the ring," Rust Hog whispered reassuringly, as Billy was about to step onto the sawdust covered floor.

"Y-Yes sir," he rasped nervously.

It seemed like a simple thing to do, and all went well until Bill got halfway around the miniature hockey rink. The four-star goat had been well fed that day and decided to take a dump when he passed by the judges stand. This wasn't a big deal in the world of long-leggedly-beasties. After all, when a critter had to, well she or he just had to. Billy stopped to let nature take its course and immediately looked around for the nearest shovel and garbage can. He spotted both and proceeded to get the flat blade from where it rested against the half-boards.

While he was bent over retrieving the pellet-like lumps, the old goat decided it was time it try out his new horns, and butted William Francis square in the rear end. Head over tea kettle took on a whole new meaning as Billy was propelled face down, his nose buried in the sawdust. Coughing up wood chips and bits of organic matter, embedded in the dusty layer, he got directly to his feet.

Young Master Carlsen was furious. He grabbed the lead rope and yanked the frothing goat swiftly towards him. A well placed fist on the creatures drippy nose established the pecking order and the rest of the showing went smoothly—much to the delight of Rust Hog and the judges.

Bill had sacrificed a few points initially for loss of control but gained a bathtub full of brownie stars for his innovative recovery. Both goat and handler were dully rewarded when the blue ribbon was announced for the event.

*

"Well done Mr. Carlsen!" The Rusty one beamed, while admiring the short, satin steamer pinned to Billy's chest.

"Thanks sir, I never thought I'd win first prize at anything in this world."

"Look here son," Dr. McTavish rumbled. "you might just have a future in An. Hub."

"No offence sir, but I've my heart set on becoming a high school teacher someday."

"Ah yes, teaching, a noble profession, I can vouch for that. Good luck to you then."

The carrot topped bull buster shook Billy's hand before going back to a front row seat right next to the judges stand.

*

William Francis was dressed in white pants, a starched white shirt, and black bow tie—the standard uniform for showing animals at College Fair. Billy desperately wanted to get out of this milkman's outfit and bolted for 301 to do a quick change. It was Thursday night and Bill was all alone. Pete had gone home for the long weekend. Experiencing a terminal attack of the lonelies, Billy went over to see what Eddie was doing. There was no answer when he knocked on his buddies door. Edward H. must have checked out of the Hereford Hilton as well. *What the heck!* He took the back steps down to the parking lot two at a time and walked purposefully towards his Rolls Royce—cleverly disguised as a '57 Chevy. Ten minutes later Billy was sitting at a table in the Empire, by himself, having a fifteen cent lager.

169

There was a prize fight on the pub's TV and Bill became engrossed in the heavyweight tilt. Suddenly he sensed that something was wrong and looked to his left. *Oh, oh, I'm in for it now.* One of Sowsburys finest was planted like a lamp post right beside his table.

"How old are you son?" The man in blue asked accusingly.

"T-Twenty-one sir," Bill squawked.

"Let's see some ID," the officer ordered threateningly.

William Francis nervously pulled out Pete's birth certficate. He grinned winningly as he handed it over. "There you go sir."

"Are you sure this is yours?" the policeman growled, fixing William Francis with a sulphurous look.

Billy knew the jig was up and what would happen next. He'd be asked for his drivers license or some other proof of age. Shaking his head slowly he decided to throw in the towel. "No sir, it's my roomies and I lied to you, I'm only twenty."

"Come with me young man," the cop snarled, while jabbing his night stick towards the door.

Once outside, the officer stood directly in front of Billy and read him the riot act. "You're under age and if I take you in, it'll be fifty bucks and twelve hours in the slammer." The imposing patrolman paused for a moment to let that sink in, then he changed tactics. "However, you were honest with me, so I'll give you a break this time, but don't let me catch you in that hotel again. Understood!"

"Y-Yes sir, thank you sir."

"Okay kid, now on your way, and remember to keep your nose clean."

Billy went directly to the parking lot behind the Empire and got into Irving. He drove carefully back to the College and headed straight for the rack.

"Maybe there really are guardian angels," he whispered happily to himself before drifting off to sleep.

33

Billy was able to keep his promise to the kindly officer who'd given him a break because the boat races were held at the Grand Central Hotel. The celebrated beer derby was one of the unofficial events of College Fair days and more popular than the Formal.

How fast you could down a glass, bottle and quart of suds had become a near Olympic event at Sowsbury. The Aggies and Vets took this competition seriously and records dated back to the beginning of time. Old Babe "Tanker Mouth" McClean, '29 V.D.C, still held the indoor record for inhaling the contents of a twelve ounce bottle in an incredible 1.5 seconds. He was considered to be a human Hoover and his amazing feat was held in awe.

*

William Francis, ignoring a twinge of guilt, entered the large convention room of the big hotel for the Friday night extravaganza. He felt sorry for Pete and Eddie who were at home on this extended weekend. Thursday had been the last day of classes, so it was really a three day rest from the rigors of lectures and labs. The university justified this short respite by designating the last day of the school week as an opportunity for students to read and study. Ho, friggin', ho.

A stage had been set up at the end of the Grand Central's capacious hall and a row of tables and chairs had been placed on the elevated platform. This sacred ground was the only place in the room where you could legally drink beer. It helped Billy with his fear of being caught in a beverage joint because he was just a member of the mob who'd gathered to cheer on the barley sandwich hopefuls.

"Hey Gary, how's it goin'?" Billy shouted over the noise of the cheering, jeering revellers.

Gary Barker was standing next to a gigantic support pillar and motioned for Bill to come over and join him.

"Your first races eh?" Gary raised his voice, while shaking Billy's hand.

"Yeah, numero uno," Bill said, happy to see his sophomore big brother.

"Have those old notes of mine been any good to you?"

"Boy, were they ever. Without them it would've been S.A.C for me."

"Sorry I haven't been over to Hereford, with hockey and everything I've been busier than a sailor in a cathouse on two for one Fridays."

"No problem," Bill chuckled appreciatively. "who's going to win the draught?"

"I'd put my money on your rugby buddy Taffy if I were you."

Before Gary could say anything else the time keepers and master of ceremonies appeared on stage. Charlie Ross carried a hefty, varnished cane and was dressed in ragged formal attire. He looked a lot like an old time chimney sweep—long scarf, top hat and work boots.

"Gentlemen!" Charlie began, no F.U.C girls were present at this hallowed stag happening. "It gives me great pleasure," he smirked, while attending to an itch slightly south of his belt buckle. "to preside over these here races. The first up will be the single glass contest."

*

One Aggie and one Vet were allowed by the rules to enter each category. The team races would come later. Taffy Morgan was squared off against Larry Dawgleish and when Charlie banged his cane on the table they grabbed their glasses.

"Down the hatch she goes and where she stops nobody knows," the big tackle bellowed.

The the four judges, two from each College, consulted their stop watches and declared that Taffy was the winner by one-tenth of a second. A thunderous cheer went up from the tractor and plough crowd. Bottles were next and Charlie relinquished his cane to Gary Barker who assumed the official starter role. Tom Grant, the Vet who'd masterminded Curtain Crashers, was Charlie's opponent.

172

Gary let drive with the polished stick of wood and before you could blink an eye the two bottles had been drained. A hush fell over the hall as the judges conferred. They handed the results to Gary and in a voice bursting with pride he announced, "Mr Ross' time gentleman, of 1.4 seconds has just established a new world record for the twelve ounce bottle."

Well, the entire planet may have been stretching it a tiny tad but the Aggies didn't care. The enormous room went wild for several minutes as the boys from the Cow College carried Charlie around the convention hall, while belting out the S.A.C fight song. It was a proud moment for all those Aggies privileged enough to see history in the making. Old Babe "Tanker Mouth" was now a fading memory, Charles Delbert Ross had just been crowned the champion of the universe. The Aggies and Vets were convinced that extraterrestrials didn't drink beer eh?

After the cheering and jeering died down Charlie, now a legend in the making, resumed his duties as ringmaster. He called for the quart contestants and once again the hardwood cane collided with the battered table top. This time it was a close one but Buffalo Bob beat the horse and dog hopeful from the V.D.C by a fraction of a second. The Vets claimed a foul bowel when Charlie foghorned a canon cracker fart just as the boys were reaching for their twenty-two ouncers. It was a clean sweep for the Aggies and there was no room for modesty; they considered themselves the best and let the opposition know it.

The team relay events were next. Each team consisted of four members and again it was glasses, bottles and quarts. Anyone who'd competed in the singles was not allowed in the team contest. The rules clearly stated that a glass of beer, or bottle had to be completely empty before the next person on the squad could begin to consume their suds. The Vets were all good at team sports and captured every category. It was now their turn for a triumphant march around the hall amid a truckload of nose rubbing. A good time was had by all. Two minutes later Charlie declared that the constest was over.

C.D. Ross, the undisputed champion of the bottle, then went on to inform the clamorous crowd that the sacred 'Boat Race Flame' would continue to burn bright until Vets and Aggies from all over the province would be called a year from this very date to compete once again. With the closing ceremonies now complete, everyone headed for the Men's beverage room of the Grand Central.

Billy, uttering a silent prayer that Officer Nice Guy wouldn't be on duty, followed the stampeding herd. All those not involved in the contest tried to make up for lost time. During the next several minutes a coalcar full of ale flowed, as free as love in Sweden, down the parched throats of the wannabe racers.

"Hey Carlsen, that was a real blast!" Charlie Ross bugled, as he plunked himself down at the table where Billy was sitting.

"Way to go Charlie, you're now the king of the brownie."

"Yeah, more like king shit of turd island," Charlie joked.

"Don't be so humble, they'll be talking about this one for years to come."

"That and a couple of dimes might get you a draught at the Empire, but it did feel good to break the record."

"You wouldn't happen to have Ellen Howard's address by any chance?" Billy asked hopefully. He'd been thinking about her a lot and knew the raven haired goddess lived in Ottawa where she and Charlie had gone to the same high school.

"Yep, not too far from my parents house. The Howard's place is at 688 Laurier Road."

"Thanks a million Charlie, I've got her phone number and Ellen told me she still lives with her mom and dad," Billy replied gratefully.

"Ellen's a real babe, but if Sandi heard that she'd have the family jewels bronzed and use them for door knockers," the big senior guffawed. "Well Billy, good luck with your quest for the Holy Quail." Charlie, listing slightly to starboard, managed to navigate a winding route across the beer hall to a table occupied by a bunch of his year '64 classmates.

The raucous group of senior Aggies were ensconced in a corner by the bar extolling the virtues of Holsteins and Udderson girls. Tit for tat as Rust Hog would say.

*

Billy had tomorrow night's Formal on his mind, and knew he'd have a fantastic time as Judy's date, but he couldn't get the alluring Ellen out of his mind. William Francis, still gun shy about being caught in the act the night before, decided to make an early exit from the suds palace. Outside in the cool, clear March air he carefully made his way to where the Chevy was parked, and once again, in a cloud of dust and a hearty Hi-ho Irving, Billy the Kid hit the trail for Hereford.

34

The President's private dining room at Hogstroff Hall was right out of a movie set. It had all the ear marks of an evening at Casa Loma, and Billy shook his head several times to convince himself that he was still in Sowsbury. The mahogany paneled walls, plush sofas, brocaded easy chairs and several Group of Seven originals, provided an atmosphere of elegance and luxury. Dry hardwood logs burned quietly in a field stone fireplace and the very best high fidelity elevator music was being piped in from heaven above. William Francis, along with three other escorts were standing near the punch bowl talking to Rust Hog. They were all decked out in rental tuxedos and pretending to enjoy the non-alcoholic, effrovescent fruit drink—pukey lime-green swamp juice, trapped in cut crystal cups.

*

Meanwhile, on the other side of the ranch, four Queen hopefuls, sequestered in separate corners, were being interviewed by the cardboard-stiff judges. It seemed like the world had started to spin backwards before the adjudicators completed their task. The head clipboard carrier finally clapped his hands to indicate that time was up. At last, the starving multitude could sit down to the loaves and fishes.

*

"What the heck's caviar?" Billy inquired quietly, shortly after they were seated at the large, oak dinning table.

"Fish eggs," Judy replied under her breath, while giving President Leonard A. Beacroft a dazzling smile.

"So that's what we were munching while you girls were at the auction," Bill replied softly, thinking the black salty spheres spread on fancy crackers weren't all that bad.

"Did you know that Dr. Beacroft's a Ph.D. in Apiculture?" Judy asked, while Billy was spooning some soup.

"You get the big one for studying apes?"

She did a double take figuring that Teddy Carlsen was kidding, but just in case. "No silly, he's a honey bee expert."

"The wonders of the natural universe will never cease to amaze me," Billy muttered. "Hey Jude, this soup's colder than Iceberg City."

"It's Vichyssoise and it's supposed to be."

"I'm almost afraid to ask," Bill whispered.

"Potatoes and white wine," Judy sighed, rolling her eyes.

"Holy mackerel, wimpy bingo and liquid spuds. You'd think that rich folks could do better than that."

Lobster à la Newberg was next followed by Beef Wellington, Yorkshire pudding, fresh vegetables, and finally Cherries Jubilee for desert. When they lit the savory fruit dish, Billy instinctively started for the fire extinguisher mounted just outside the door. Judy grabbed his wrist firmly and hissed, "It's only a tablespoon of brandy being flamed for the effect."

"Boy, is that ever a waste of good booze," Billy mimicked, conjuring up a misty apparition of Jackie Gleason, leaning against the mantel of the cheery fireplace.

Judy groaned, but put her best look forward as she eyed and beguiled each of the judges in turn. She had that come hither look and was exploiting it to her best advantage. Judy had a figure that wouldn't quit, so maybe there was a glimmer. After all, the panel was made up exclusively of card carrying males who's hockey sticks had been hard-wired, in a stroke of evolutionary genius, to by-pass the cerebral cortex.

*

The dinner now over, each of the Queen hopefuls followed their escorts to the various and assorted chariots that would carry them to the Physical Education's elaborately decorated grand ballroom, where the Formal's hoofer and stomper was being held. In other words: down in the Boy's Gym, or perhaps the female equivalent depending on your misty memories of the sizzling sixties.

"I don't have a chance," Judy groused, once they were safely in Iriving's cosy confines. "Did you see Donna's dress and all that cleavage? Old Beacroft had to defog his glasses several times before he could write anything at all."

"Yeah, but I was watching the judges closely, and I think they voted for you as the most alluring of the group."

"Is that a polite term for sexy?"

"You betcha!" Billy smiled, as he pulled into the drop off area in front to the jock's glitter dome.

*

The feature attraction was the Big Band sound of the forties. This satisfied the Profs. and their wives, along with most of the students who were born during the war. *That's the Second, in case you were wondering. There sure were some notable ones during the twentieth.*

Billy was looking forward to hearing the Glenn Miller band conducted by Ray McKinnley. He'd been to one of their shows in Bala during the summer of '61 and was very fond of the Miller style. Bill was also pleased to find out that David Clayton-Thomas and The Fabulous Shays were the backup group. William Francis knew David Clayton from Johnnies Surf Club in Port Carter. Some of sweetness rock 'n' roll this side of heaven was in store for the folks at the Formal.

"Boy, "In The Mood's" still one of the best for doing the boogie woogie," Judy gushed when the Miller orchestra had finished their first set.

"Yeah, but wait until you hear Davy C. and his sidemen."

Several minutes later, Clayton-Thomas marched across the stage, thanked the audience for their warm welcome, then exploded into his hit record, 'Boom Boom". *A real catchy tile eh?* The senior staff sat out the rock tunes while the kids from Sow U went ballistic on the hardwood. It was the perfect mix of old and new. By the time the judges were called upon to announce the Queen of the corn field, all those present were in need of a visit to cooler pastures.

*

"Ladies and Gentlemen, your attention please," President Beacroft modulated in deep resonant tones, he then paused momentarily for effect. "I'm proud to announce," the Miller band drummer provided a perfunctory roll. "that the Queen of the Formal is; Miss Judy Lawson."

Billy was stunned and of course Judy was flabbergasted. She wasn't expecting it and her look of total surprise was genuine. She moved slowly towards the stage and was escorted to the royal throne by a grinning Dean Angus. The old dirt Doc's hands were hardpan steady when he placed the glittering tiara on Judy's head. Flanked by the three runner's-up, each one fighting a losing battle to look like a good sport, Judy smiled regally as the official photographer got off more shots than a legion of duck hunters on opening day. Several moments later Judy and Billy whirled across the highly polished basketball court, during 'the Queen's dance', to the soft strains of "Moonlight Serenade". They moved well together, a fairy tale come true in living colour. The sideline couples eventually joined in and the rest of the evening evaporated like dry ice on a wet July morning.

*

The post prom shindig was held at the Sowsbury Motor Hotel. Billy had booked a room but never in his wildest did he think he'd be spending the night with the Queen of the castle. The festivities moved like a wave from room to room and gallons of booze gouged deep rivers in the parched throats of the party hardy crowd.

Charlie Ross was in good form and jumped naked into the hotel's indoor pool. The girls applauded loudly when he emerged from the crystal clear, chlorinated waters. Fifty virginal daughters of the F.U.C. sighed in unison when they viewed his larger than life attributes.

The bash crashed loudly with the mystical pre-dawn light. Strolling sleepily, in the magic moments of a glowing red sunrise, Queen Judy and her Royal Consort retired to their regal chambers.

"You're so lovely," William Francis murmured as he helped Judy out her full length, gold lame evening gown. The black nylons and lacy garter belt she modeled for him were straight out of a *Playboy* centerfold.

"Well Prince Charming," Judy giggled, "it's time for all good Aggies to seek repose with the woman of their dreams."

Billy gulped noisily, mesmerized by the gorgeous creature laying spread eagle on the starched, white sheets. At that precise moment Teddy Carlsen, while staring downward at his barefeet, realized that he and the rising sun definitely had something in common.

180

35

College Fair days were history and it was business as usual at the horse barns. Billy hadn't heard from Judy all week and wasn't surprised when he saw her with Jimmy Jones the richest Aggie on campus. His father owned the G.B. Jones Jam Company and young James was his only son. The overtures of sticky fingers Jim, a prime catch, had inspired Judy, the Queen of all she surveyed, to make the most out of her new found fame. When they drove by in Jimmy's new Corvette she presented Billy with a regal wave—her farewell gesture to the former King of the ball. "I hope she chokes on a Jones Jelly Roll," William Francis muttered, as the souped up Vette entered the parking lot beside Hogstroff Hall.

*

He'd been dropped like a hot horseshoe, but that was only a blow to his ego. Next Monday would be April fools day and final exams were a peripheral white dot on the radar scope. Billy, like the raw-assed butcher who'd gotten a little behind in his work, really didn't have the luxury to feel sorry for himself. Squaring his shoulders, and with a quivering lower lip, he walked purposefully back to Hereford.

*

"Hey Carlsen there's a call for you," Eddie hollered, while Billy was coming up the hallway to 301.

"Who is it?"

"Some babe lover boy." Ed humped the air suggestively, as Bill drew nearer.

Following a playful jab at Eddie's left shoulder, Billy grabbed the phone and managed a hesitant, "He-Hello."

"It's Ellen Billy."

For a moment it didn't register, but regaining his composure he squeaked, "How are things on parliament hill?"

"Beats me, because I'm right here in Sowsbury."

"Wow! Is that ever groovy. When did you arrive?"

"A week ago, but this is the first free time I've had since I got off the bus."

"Didn't you have a job in Ottawa?" Billy asked.

"I did, but I'm now the Charge Technician in Bacteriology at Saint Al's. Sister Florence retired and the Head of Laboritories was impressed by my performance when I was taking the course here, so she offered me the position."

"Hey, way to go. Is there any chance we can get together to celebrate."

"Let's see, it's Thursday and I'm on-call till Sunday morning at ten."

"Okay then, I'll pick you up at noon on Sunday and we'll go for a drive."

"That sounds like fun. I'll see you soon Billy."

He stood there for a minute after hanging up the phone and couldn't believe what had just happened. William Francis hurried to his room, flopped on the narrow single and blew out a king-sized breath.

"You all right Billy?" Pete looked concerned.

"Roger that. All systems are A-okay," William Francis modulated in his best John Glenn imitation

"So what's up?"

"The fairy Princess just arrived from the enchanted kingdom," Billy murmured blissfully.

The sidewalks were rolled up on Sunday in Sowsbury, therefore, the proverbial drive was a great way to spend an afternoon. Billy and Ellen motored into the back farm country. Patchy snow dotting the muddy, ploughed fields was a sure sign that spring had finally arrived. William Francis spotted a producing sugar maple bush and stopped the car. They bailed out of Irving, then headed for the log sided sugar shack—a snaking cloud of white smoke drifting upwards from the evaporator. If their luck held, they'd be able to purchase a quart or two of maple syrup directly from the source.

A wind burned, jack shirted farmer met the young couple in front of the rough hewed building and welcomed them to his farm. "How're ya t-day," he rasped, through a set of clenched teeth that had fended off the wind and cold of many a hard winter.

He'd just boiled off twenty gallons and was glad for the business. Ellen and Billy pooled their resources and managed to assemble enough coin of the realm to buy two quarts of commercial grade syrup. The real dark stuff had the best maple flavour.

"It's been one of 'ur finer runs," the farmer whistled through a missing tooth, while inserting a tarnished, metal funnel into a forty ounce can. "The warm sunny days, like right now, and cold nights have been a real blessing."

"How many trees have you got tapped?" Ellen asked.

"Bout fifteen-hundred," the ruddy cheeked syrup merchant answered proudly.

"Boy, that sure is a lot of pails," Billy marvelled.

"Yep, and don't I know it, me and the wife have to clean everyone of 'em when the runs over. It's a lot of work so it t'is, but it gives us some ready cash to buy corn seed."

This part of Cowplop Township was settled by the Northern Irish and some of the old country lilt could still be heard. It was good rich farmland but required gut busting labour to reap its benefits. Billy had a fantasy of getting back to the land but this visit was an instant reality check. He realized, after talking to the farmer, how difficult it was to make a living in agriculture. The freedom was there, but a dawn to dusk effort was required each and every day.

"It's been a pleasure meetin' you young feller and you as well miss," the landowner said cheerfully, just before Bill and Ellen were about to leave.

Billy nodded, as he spontaneously placed his arm around Ellen's shoulders. "Best of luck with the corn sir."

The farmer stroked his chin knowingly. "Well, one thing fer sure, we won't put 'er in till the frogs close three times."

"That's what they say in the Ottawa Valley too," Ellen paused, remembering some eastern Ontario folklore. "and don't plant your tomatoes till after the first full moon in June."

"You'd make a good farmer there young lady, so you would," the Cowplop syrup seller chorteled softly.

"Thanks again sir, and I'm going to have some of this liquid gold on a big piece of rhubarb pie that my grandma just sent me," Billy stated wistfully, before they strolled back to where the Bel Air was parked. Granny McNair from time to time would send Bill a care package and this last one had contained a pie and a trunk load of brownies. She still thought he looked a little thin, and they weren't feeding him enough up at that college.

*

The drive back to St. Alfreds was full of promise, a mirror image of the softening March sunshine that warmed the land. The Robins were back, but the doom and gloomers were predicting one last winter's storm in honour of the red breasts return. This was another piece of Upper Canada superstition that had been firmly entrenched since the days of Laura Secord, but damn it all, she did make mighty fine chocolates.

*

When they pulled into the hospital's parking lot Ellen leaned over and kissed Billy full on the mouth. "This has been a magic time and I really don't want it to end just yet," she purred musically.

" W-Well, Miss," Billy sputtered, "we could always find a nice quiet place to park and discuss the deepening mysteries of the Big Bang Theory."

"I've got a better idea. Sister Mary Margaret, my roommate's away for the weekend, so we could have our little talk upstairs," Ellen cooed, while pointing to the top floor of the nurses residence.

"Sounds like a winner to me." Billy's heart did a backflip, as his mind slammed into fast-forward—conjuring up several delicious, romantic possibilities.

*

The room was much like the cubicle he shared with Pete. Two single beds, two desks and two dressers. Even the cast iron steam registers were painted the same, dull-as-dishwater, battleship grey.

184

"Boy, you sure have some snazzy digs," Billy said, while tilting back in the straight backed chair adjacent to Ellen's mission oak desk. The room had been tastefully furnished in early sally ann.

"Yes, Sister Mary Margaret and me self, as she would say, are reasonably comfortable here."

Ellen was sitting on her bed and patted a spot next to her left thigh and said, "You look a little lonely over there, so why don't you sit beside me."

*

His world was going from good to gooder. They small talked for several minutes but all went silent when their lips finally met. He pulled a clever reach for the shoulder move but this was only a feint as he stealthily encountered a firm, ripe, right breast. He wasn't admonished for having wandering hand trouble and proceeded with basic exploration tactics. Billy was successfully inching his way towards third base when the phone rang. Ellen disengaged reluctantly and picked up the receiver. After a short series of yes's and okays she laid the phone back onto it's cradle.

"Sister Florence is coming up to see me," Ellen gasped, seeming to be in a state of panic.

Billy smiled innocently. "Gee, I'd really like to meet her."

"Th-there's one small thing I forgot to tell you. We're not supposed to have men in our rooms."

"Oh," he groaned loudly. *Holy smokers, I should've twigged on that one. Sister Mary Margaret's my roomie and Bob's your uncle. Come on Carlsen time to flew the coop.*

"Billy, there's a way out of this mess, Mary Margaret's a rather large woman and I'll bet you'd fit her habit perfectly."

"Not a snowballs chance, lately I've been trying hard to kick the habit," he smart-alecked, trying to lighten things up.

Ellen couldn't suppress a fit of the giggles but two minutes later she had William Francis decked out in a penguins uniform that would have convinced a New York audience that he was about to go on stage as a star performer in the "Sound of Music".

185

"Now remember, if we meet Sister Florence on the way out of here, keep mum."

"Gottcha," Billy chuckled, beginning to enjoy his role as Mrs. Dress Up.

They'd made it partway down the stairs and thought the coast was clear until Ellen spotted Sister Florence rounding the second floor landing. It was too late for a retreat.

"Oh, hello Sister," Ellen quavered, when they met between the third and second. "Mary Margaret isn't feeling well and I was just taking her down to Emerg."

"May the Saints preserve us. Is there anything I can do to help."

"No, we'll be okay. You go on up to my room and I'll be back shortly."

Considering the situation, it was a just as well that dear, longer in the tooth Sister Florence was developing cataracts in both eyes and was hard of hearing. She did, however, look deeply concerned when Billy hammed it up by letting out a low-pitched moan a second after Ellen mentioned that her roommate was on the slippery slope of declining health.

Once they'd reached the parking lot Ellen's pulse rate slowed to normal.

"Billy, if you can, return the habit to me before midnight. I just hope that Sister Florence doesn't find out that Mary Margaret's away."

"You can count on the glad rags being here this evening. Boy, there's one thing you can say about today, it's sure been exciting."

"Good-bye for now," she whispered, "and please leave me a package at the front desk before the bewitching hour."

"No problemo," Billy reassured, as he climbed into Irving.

*

On the drive back to the campus Bill suddenly realized how he was dressed. He'd gotten a number of curious stares from passing motorists, and decided to pull into a gas station to change. Fortunately the washroom wasn't locked and Billy was able to pull a Superman operation in record time.

While in costume William Francis felt a lot like the fourth selection on a multiple choice test. *Yep, you guessed it, Nun of the above. Possibly he'd just passed into the Twilight Zone and was now Saint Francis of SAC or some quaint Italian town with a similar sounding name. No diagrams required eh?*

*

When Billy got back to Hereford he neatly bundled up Mary Margaret's clothes in a large sheet of gift wrapping paper, saved from one of Granny McNair's care packages, and carefully tied it with binder twine. At nine o'clock Bill drove back to the hospital and asked the nice girl at the receptionists desk if she'd be kind enough to phone Ellen Howard and tell her that the parcel she'd been expecting had arrived.

*

Pete had already hit the sack and was snoring softly as Teddy the former nunny bunny walked quietly into 301. He was bushed and sleep came easily.

187

36

The crunch was on. Finals were written during the last two weeks in April and Billy figured he didn't have a prayer. He'd tried his best but a short, meteoric ride at Sow U was about to hit the atmosphere with a dazzling shower of sparkles.

Each paper Bill sat for was a three hour endurance contest and he felt like a punch drunk fighter when the last exam had been written.

*

"So what's up for the summer?" Eddie asked, as he helped Billy load his gear into Irving, the morning after the year end bash at the Empire.

"Beats me, I've been too damn busy trying to survive."

"Not to worry Carlsen, second year's waiting out there at centre ice for the good guys."

"I sure wish I had your confidence Eddie."

"It'll all be roses and lollipops Billy, and remember you me and Pete are going to rent that babe catcher over on Bovine Boulevard, so you'd better make it back."

Before the exams began Bill, Ed and Pete had looked at a three bedroom apartment not too far from the University. They'd signed a lease to start in September and had laid down seventy-five pictures of her Royal Majesty in order to hold it for the fall. Billy wasn't all that sure he'd be able to join his pals come the smoky days preceding the autumnal equinox.

"Say Eddie, there's a pub called the Hollywood House in Norval near Georgetown. When I get a job and settled back home, I'll give you a shout on the landline. We'll get together for a couple of ales and you can stay over at our place for a weekend."

"Sounds great Billy. Well, it's good-bye for now, but stay in touch eh?'

"Will do my friend."

Bill was just about to get into the Chevy when Pete trotted across the parking lot.

"See ya after the summer holidays Billy," Good Aggie Eastman panted, slightly out of breath.

"Yeah, and we'll have a real blast over there on Bovine."

"Well you two will, but I'm sticking with Tova. She just read an article about girls from Denmark who are convinced that premarital is the only way to fly. I think my life's going to get a little more interesting when we return to the Cow College."

"Remember, no heavy breathing from the cheap seats," Eddie chimed in.

Pete extended his hand to Bill and stage whispered, "Catch ya later Mule."

"Not if I spot you first Spin," Billy retorted, remembering their first days as roomies.

"Is that some sort of private joke?" Eddie asked.

"You betcha!" William Francis smirked, while shutting the door of the Bel Air.

"Take care Carlsen," Pete shouted, as Bill slowly pulled away from the parking lot at the rear of Hereford.

*

Eight months had evaporated in a single blink. Life seemed to be that way. You waited for things that took forever to happen, then suddenly they disappeared in a wisp of nostalgic mist. "I guess at the end it'll be like that," William Francis mused out loud. "You'll look back and the trail behind will have vanished." *An impartial ocean streaming across the rippling sands to wash away your footprints.*

Halfway home, Iriving began to sputter and wheeze, then with a horrific backfire, the well worn chunk of Detroit iron quit like an old horse on a one-way to the glue factory. Billy gingerly lifted the hood expecting to see a collection of battered nuts and bolts. All appeared to be normal and he couldn't figure out what was wrong. William Francis was so intent on trouble shooting the engine failure that he didn't notice the man standing beside him.

"What seems to be the problem?" a loudspeaker voice rumbled directly next to Billy's left ear.

"Holy shit!" Bill jumped back reflexively, before noticing a friendly face smiling at him.

"Sorry son," I didn't mean to give you a start but I owned a '57 several years back, maybe I can help."

The booming baritone was attached to a middle aged, slightly balding man who looked a lot like Alfred Hitchcock.

"Th-That would be much appreciated," Billy stuttered, slowly beginning to regain his composure.

The portly stranger carefully inspected the inline six and began to stroke his chin. "It's the distributor, the collar's loose and the timing's way off."

"Can you fix it?" Billy half pleaded.

"Sure can," the good Samaritan answered confidently, as he headed towards his '64 Fairlane to retrieve the required tools.

When he returned, crescent wrench and screwdriver in hand, Billy knew from helping his dad that they'd have to rotate the distributor and tighten it in place so the engine would turn over and start.

"I understand now sir, but won't we need a timing light to set things up."

"Nope, I've done enough of these on my old car to know the approximate position, after that we'll fine tune her by ear."

Several minutes later Irving was purring like a cat who'd moved to Mouseville and Billy was ready to continue his journey. Just before he put in the clutch the stranger, now standing next to the drivers side window, smiled before saying, "By the way my name's Bruce Willmen."

Bill extended his hand and grasped the over sized bear paw that was offered in return.

"Billy Carlsen sir," he replied thankfully.

"Where are you headed Billy?"

"Georgetown, I just finished up at Sowsbury Agricultural College and I'm on my way home for the summer."

"You got a job yet son?"

"No sir, but I'll be looking for one the first of next week."

"Well, maybe I can help you out. I'm a Civil Engineer for Klein Brothers in Brampton and we need a chainman for our survey crew."

"Holy smoke, I'd love to have a job like that!" Billy bluffed, not really knowing what a chainman was. It sounded like something out of a swampy prison flick—Tony Curtis and Sydney Poitier being chased by a hollowing pack of drooling, flop-eared bloodhounds.

"If you're serious, then report to our office on Highway 10 Monday morning. The salary's sixty a week."

Billy gripped the steering wheel in order to steady himself. He was sure that old man Montroy would hire him at Canada Tire in Gerorgetown, but he knew from his high school days that a buck an hour would be tops. Here was someone offering him a whole lot more for a job in the great outdoors. He shot his hand out again and managed to rasp, "It's a deal Mr. Willmen, I'll be front and centre when your office opens."

"Okay then Billy, we'll see you the first of the week."

The rotund engineer waved good-bye and got into his Fairlane. He pulled out from behind the Chevy and disappeared around a bend in the road before Billy was able to get the cobwebs clear from his brain. Just like that he'd landed gainful employment at a wage that was on the fat side of easy streets. Bill knew for a fact that ladies working at the local Chainway were only making fifty cents an hour. Hell, he could get more than that baby sitting. From now on he'd have to pay attention to his mom when she talked about the pitifully poor hourly rates being doled out to the women of the country. She would have made a good union type but she had a family to raise and accepted the fact that she was being paid about half what a man would get for doing the same job at the municipal offices in Georgetown. His mother was a battler though, Barbara Carlsen headed the local chapter of 'Women For Coloured Margarine'. She considered the bubble on the Blue Bonnet package you had to squeeze in order to colour the gummy, white stuff, a travesty of justice. Mrs. Carlsen was no shrinking violet!

Billy arrived home just in time for supper and was greeted like a sailor returning from a long voyage. His mother, grandmother and sister were overjoyed to see him. Mr. Carlsen was working the afternoon shift and wouldn't be home until midnight.

*

After a welcome back dinner of mock duck, canned peas and fried potatoes Billy went down to the rec-room to watch game six of the Stanley cup final. The leafs had squeaked by Montreal in a game seven semi, where Dave Keon had scored all the goals and were now up against it with Detroit who led the series three games to two. This was a different team from the start of the season. In January Punch Imlach had traded Dick Duff and Bob Nevin to the Rangers for Andy Bathgate and Don McKenny.

*

At the end of regulation the game was tied. Things looked bad for the Leafs because Bobby Baun, their star blueliner, had gone off in the third with what appeared to be broken ankle. It seemed like a miracle when Baun came out for the overtime period and even more miraculous when he scored the winner. Later it was leaked to the press that Baun's ankle was indeed broken but he'd been shot up with novocaine and was able to skate. The hard nosed defenceman would become a living legend for his performance that night.

*

Saturday night, Hockey Night in Canada and game seven of the Cup final. It doesn't get better than that eh? Ours back's are up against the wall, there's no tomorrow, everyone has to give one-hundred and ten percent. All the cliches had be espoused by the players on both sides as Bill and his dad settled in to watch the last match of the NHL season. Andy Bathgate scored the first goal and that's all it took as the Toronto Maple Leafs skunked the Detroit Red Wings four zip. Punch Imlach, the much criticized coach of the Leafs, was hailed as a genius. The Buds had managed a three-peat and there was joy in Hogtown. It was April the 25th, 1964.

Billy went up to his room after the Juliette show. He was home, had completed his first year, had a summer job and his favorite team had come through in a fairy tale finish. Life was good. If the academic gods were kind to him, he might sneak by into second year. Bill had called Ellen in the afternoon and she was looking forward to seeing him next weekend. Three more years at the Cow College would be sweeter than a banana split at the Tasty Freeze. A pink, puffy cloud thought drifted across his half-awake brain just before he went lights out. If his dream of becoming a teacher came true, then during the ebb and flood of many a tide, for this collection of living cells, travelling on a planet, hurtling through space about a life giving star, in a universe substantially larger than a bread basket, between summers there would always be school. *To everything there is a season, a time for every purpose under heaven.*

Epilogue:

William Francis did manage to pass all his exams and an honours grade in Animal Hubandry put him over the sixty bar. Rust Hog was now on his official guardian angels list. The reality was, however, that Billy had barely squeaked through, but a pass was a pass. He berated himself for not trying harder and doing better, but then he remembered what his Uncle Ole would have said: "Ya can't tire patch the past but ya sure can blow out 'ur day by rubber-necking around in the what ifs, should'ves and could'ves of back down the road." *Time capsules eh?*

Billy dated Ellen on a regular basis during the summer of '64 and they were starting to become a number. The future was out there bright and shining for young Master Carlsen and all systems were go.

*

In the fullness of time Billy did get his Aggie degree and landed a job with Ross Bradley at good old Fowler. Bill would be the first to admit that attending the Cow College was the most important decision of his life. Eddie surprised everyone by going on to Osgoode Hall before opening a very successful law practice in his hometown. Pete and Tova got hitched shortly after they finished at Bible College and served as missionaries in deepest, darkest downtown Toronto. Gary Barker received his iron ring and Charlie Ross raised prize Hereford beef cattle. Doc Livingstone, while water skiing down the Mississippi, met the lady owner of a casino boat and eventually became an accomplished black jack dealer. Tex Graham, after graduating from Ryerson, went into business for himself as an insurance broker. Taffy Morgan returned to Wales and taught at an Agricultural College. He also coached their rugger team.

Donna Parker and Judy Lawson traded in their Home Ec. degrees for the coveted MRS. Donna married Larry and Judy tied the knot with old sticky fingers Jim. And what of Ellen Howard? She married Billy of course and they lived happily ever after.

Exit Satchmo playing,
Upbeat on your feet.
"When Those Saints
Go Marching In".

Out of sight Daddio,
I heard it on the Raddio.

That's all folks!